George Manville Fenn

King of the Castle

A novel. Vol. 1

George Manville Fenn

King of the Castle
A novel. Vol. 1

ISBN/EAN: 9783337065898

Printed in Europe, USA, Canada, Australia, Japan

Cover: Foto ©Andreas Hilbeck / pixelio.de

More available books at **www.hansebooks.com**

King of the Castle.

A NOVEL

BY

G. MANVILLE FENN,

AUTHOR OF

'THIS MAN'S WIFE;' 'THE MASTER OF THE CEREMONIES;'
'DOUBLE CUNNING,' ETC., ETC.

IN THREE VOLUMES.

VOL. I.

LONDON:

WARD & DOWNEY,

12 YORK STREET, COVENT GARDEN.

———

1892.

CONTENTS.

⎯⎯◆⎯⎯

CHAPTER IX.

CHAPTER X.

CHAPTER XI.

CHAPTER XII.

CHAPTER XIII.

CHAPTER XIV.

CHAPTER XV.

CHAPTER XVI.

KING OF THE CASTLE

KING OF THE CASTLE.

CHAPTER I.

PART OF THE GARRISON.

"HULLO, Claude, going for a walk?"

"Yes, papa."

"Alone?"

"No: Mary is going with me."

"Humph! If you were as giddy as Mary, I'd—I'd—"

"What, papa?"

"Don't know; something bad. But, Claude, my girl."

"Yes, dear?"

"Why the dickens don't you dress better? Look at you!"

The girl admonished turned merrily round, and stood facing an old bevelled-glass cabinet in the solid-looking, well-furnished library, and saw her reflection—one which for some reason made her colour slightly; perhaps with pleasure at seeing her handsome oval face with soft, deep brown hair, and large dark, well-shaded eyes—a face that needed no more display to set it off than the plain green cloth well-fitting dress, held at the throat by a dead gold brooch of Roman make.

"Well, papa," she said, as she altered the sit of her natty, flat-brimmed straw hat, "what is the matter with my dress?"

The big-headed, grey-haired man addressed gave his stiff, wavy locks an impatient rub, wrinkled his broad forehead, and then smiled in a happy, satisfied way, his dark eyes lighting up, and his smile driving away the hard, severe look which generally rested upon his brow.

"The matter?" he said, drawing the girl on to his knee and kissing her. "I don't understand such things; but your dress seems too common and plain."

"But one can't wear silks and satins and muslins to scramble among the rocks and go up the glen."

"Well, there, don't bother me. But dress

better. If you want more money you can have it. You ought to take the lead here, and there were ladies on some of the yachts and on the pier yesterday who quite left you behind.—Yes! What is it?"

"Isaac Woodham, from the quarry, sir, would like to see you," said a servant.

"Confound Isaac Woodham! Send him in."

The servant retired, leaving his master muttering.

"Wants to spend money in some confounded new machinery or something. I made all my money without machinery, Claude, but these people want to waste it with their new-fangled plans."

"But, papa dear, do speak more gently to them."

"What! let them be masters and eat me out of house and home? Not such a fool."

"But, papa—"

"Hold your tongue. Weak little goose. You don't know them; I do. They must be ruled—ruled. There: be off, and get your walk. Seen Mr Glyddyr to-day?"

The girl flushed scarlet.

" Hallo, pussy ; that brings the colour to your cheeks."

" No, papa ; indeed I—"

" Yes, I know. I say, Claudie, fine handsome fellow, eh ? Bit too pale for a yachtsman. But what a yacht ! Do you know he came in for three hundred and fifty thousand when his father died ?"

" Indeed, papa ?" said the girl carelessly.

" Yes ! Old Glyddyr was not like your grandfather, confound him."

" Papa ! "

" Con—found him ! Didn't I speak plain? Glyddyr left his boys a slate quarry in Wales for the eldest, and three hundred and fifty for the younger. Parry's the younger. Eh ? Nice fortune for a handsome young yachtsman, Claudie. There, go and have your walk, and keep Mary out of mischief.—Well ? "

This was to a hard, heavy-looking man in working clothes, covered with earth stains and stone dust, who was ushered into the room, and who, ignoring the speaker's presence, stood bowing awkwardly, cap in hand, and changing it from right to left and back.

"Quite well, thank ye, miss, and sent her dooty to you."

"I'm very glad, Woodham. Remember me kindly to Sarah, and tell her I shall call at the cottage soon."

"Yes, yes," said the old man impatiently, following his daughter to the door; "go on now. I have business with Woodham. Don't be so familiar with the work-people," he whispered, as he closed the door after the girl, who ran lightly to the foot of the great carved oak staircase, to call out merrily,—

"Not ready, Mary?"

"Yes; coming, coming, coming," and a quaint, mischievous-looking little body came tripping down the stairs, halting slightly as if from some form of lameness, which her activity partly concealed. But no effort or trick of dress could hide the fact that she was deformed, stunted in proportion, and with her head resting closely between her shoulders, which she had a habit of shrugging impatiently when addressed.

"Oh, do make haste, Mary, or we shall have no time before lunch."

"Yes, I know. You've seen him go by."

"For shame, Mary!" said Claude, flushing. "You are always thinking of such things. It is not true."

"Yes, it is; and I don't think more of such things than you do. 'Oh, 'tis love, 'tis love, 'tis love that makes the world go round,'" she sang, in a singularly sweet, thrilling soprano voice, her pretty but thin keen face lighting up with a malicious smile. But the old song was checked by Claude's hand being clapped sharply over her mouth.

"Be quiet, and come along. Papa will hear you."

"Well, I daresay he wants to see his darling married. Take away your hand, or I'll bite it."

"You're in one of your mocking moods this morning, Mary, and you really make me hate you."

"Don't tell fibs," said the deformed girl, throwing her arms lovingly about her companion. "You couldn't hate anybody, you dear old pet; and why shouldn't you have a true, handsome lover?"

"Oh, Mary, you are insufferable. You think of nothing else but lovers."

"Well, why not, Claudie?" said the girl with a sigh, and a peculiarly pinched look coming about her mouth, as her clear, white forehead wrinkled up, and her fine eyes seemed full of trouble. "One always longs for the un-attainable. Nobody will ever love me, so why shouldn't I enjoy seeing somebody love you?"

"Mary, darling, I love you dearly."

"Yes, pet, like the dearest, sweetest old sister that ever was. You worship poor old humpty dumpty?"

"Don't ridicule yourself, Mary dear."

"Why not? But I meant no nice, hand-some Christopher Lisle will ever want to look in my eyes and say—"

"Will you be quiet, Mary? Why will you be always bringing up Mr Christopher Lisle? I never tease you about Mr Gullick."

"Because—because—because—"

She did not finish her speech, but burst out into a loud, ringing laugh, full of teasing, malicious mirth, till she saw Claude's flushed face, and then she stopped short.

"There, I've done. Which way shall we go?"

"I don't care. I feel as if I'd rather stay at home now."

"No, no; I won't tease. Shall we go as far as the town?"

"No; anywhere you like."

"Say somewhere."

"Not I. You'll only tease me, and say I had some reason. I'll only go where you choose."

"Then you shall, dear. We'll go up the east glen to the fall, and then cross over the hill and come back by the west glen, and you shall tease me as much as you like."

"I don't want to tease you."

Mary made a grimace as she looked sidewise at herself, but she coloured a little, and was silent for a time.

They were already some hundred yards from the great, grey granite mansion, which stood upon a bald bluff of cliff, built within the past thirty years, and by the fancy of its architect made to resemble a stronghold of the Norman times, with its battlements, towers, frowning gateway, moat and drawbridge crossing the deep channel, kept well filled by a spring far up in one of the glens at the back, while the front of the solid-looking, impregnable edifice frowned down upon the glittering sea.

"See how grand Castle Dangerous looks from here," said Mary Dillon, as they were about to turn up the glen. "Don't you often feel as if we were two forlorn maidens—I mean," she cried merrily, "a forlorn maiden and a half—shut up in that terrible place waiting for a gallant knight and a half to come and rescue us from the clutches of ogre-like Uncle Gartram?"

"Mary, darling," said Claude affectionately, "if you knew how you hurt me, you would cease these mocking allusions to your affliction."

"Then I will not hurt you any more, pet. But I am such a sight."

"No, you are not. You have, when in repose, the sweetest, cleverest face I ever saw."

"Let's be in repose, then."

"And you know you are brilliant in intellect, where I am stupid."

"Oh! if I could be as stupid!"

" And you have the sweetest voice possible.
See what gifts these are."

" Oh, yes, I suppose so, Claudie, but I don't
care for them a bit—not a millionth part as
much as having your love. There, don't let's
talk nonsense. Come along."

She hurried her companion over a bridge
and towards a path roughly made beside the
babbling stream which supplied the moat at
the Fort, and then in and out among the rocks,
and beneath the pensile birches which shed a
dappled shade over the path, while every
here and there in gardens great clumps of
fuchsias and hydrangeas showed the moist
warmth of the sheltered nook.

They walked quickly, Claude urged on by
her companion, who climbed the steep path
with the agility of a goat, till they reached a
fall, where the water came tumbling over the
hoary, weather-stained rocks, and the path
forked, one track going over the stream behind
the fall, and the other becoming a rough stair-
way right up the side of the glen.

" Hadn't we better go this way ? " said
Claude timidly, indicating the route to the left.

"No; too far round," said Mary peremptorily. "Come along," and she began to skip from rock to rock and rough step to step, up the side of the glen, Claude following her with more effort till they reached the rugged top of the cliff, and continued their walk onward among heather bloom and patches of beautifully fine grass, with here and there broken banks, where the wild thyme made the air fragrant with its scent.

"This is ten times as nice as going through the woods," cried Mary. "You seem to get such delicious puffs of the sea breeze. *Vorwarts!*"

She hurried her companion on for about a mile, when the track turned sharply off to the right, and a steep descent led them to the banks of another stream which was gradually converging towards the one they had left, so that the two nearly joined where they swept down their rocky channels into the sea.

"This is ten times as good a way, Claudie. I always think it is the prettiest walk we have. Look what a colour the fir trees are turning, with those pale green tassels at the

tips; and how beautiful those patches of gorse
are. I wish one could get such a colour in
paintings."

She chatted on merrily as they descended
the stream, with its many turns and zigzags,
through the deep chasm along which it ran;
and whenever Claude appeared disposed to
speak, Mary always had some familiar object
to which she could draw her companion's
attention. In fact, it seemed as if she would
not give her time to think, as she noted that
a quick, nervous look was directed at the
stream from time to time.

A stranger might have thought Claude was
nervous about the risks of the path as it went
round some pool, with the rocks coming down
perpendicularly to the deep, dark water. Or
that she was in dread of encountering graver
difficulties in the lonely ravine, whose almost
perpendicular sides were clothed with growth
of a hundred tints. Far beneath them, flashing, foaming, and hurrying on with a deep,
murmuring sound, ran the little river, from
rapid to fall, and from fall to deep, dark, slug-
gish-looking hole; while in places the trees,

which had contrived to get a footing in some crevice of the rock, overhung the river, and threw the water beneath into the deepest shade.

They reached, at length, a more open part, where the sun shone down brightly, and their way lay through a patch of moss-grown hazel stubbs, which after a few steps made a complete screen from the sun's rays, and they walked over a verdant carpet which silenced every footfall.

"We shall have plenty of time," said Mary, as they reached the farther edge of the hazel clump, "and we may as well sit down on the rocks and read."

"No, not now," said Claude hastily. Then in an agitated whisper, as a peculiar whizzing noise was heard: "Oh, Mary, this is too cruel. Why have you brought me here?"

"Because it was not considered good for Adam to live alone in Paradise. There's poor Adam alone and disconsolate, fishing to pass time away. Paradise in the glen is very pretty, but dull. Enter Eve. Now, Claude, dear, show yourself worthy of the name of woman. Go on!"

CHAPTER II.

Norman Gartram returned to his seat, looking rigid and scowling as he gazed fiercely at the workman.

"Well?" he said sharply.

"Don't believe she can be his bairn," said the workman to himself, as he returned his employer's angry stare.

"I said *Well!*"

"I heard you, master. Needn't shout."

"What do you want?"

"Come about the big block at the corner. Time it was blasted down."

"Then blast it down; and how many more times am I to tell you to say *sir* to me?"

"You're my master, and pay me my wage, and I earn it honest. That's all there is between us, for the Lord made all men equal, and—"

"Look here, Isaac Woodham, once for all I

14

will not have any of your Little Bethel caut in my presence. Now about this block ; let it be deeply tamped, and the powder put well home."

"I'm going to blast it down with dinnymite."

The elder man flushed up scarlet, and the veins in his forehead swelled up into knotted network.

"Once for all—" he thundered.

"There, don't get in a way, master," said the man coolly. "If you go on like that you'll be having another fit, and I'm sure you oughtn't to cut short such a life as yours."

"Isaac Woodham, one of these days you'll tempt me to knock you down. Insolent brute ! And now, look here ; I've told you before that I would not have dynamite used in my quarry. I'll have my work done as it always has been done—with powder. The first man who uses a charge of that cursed stuff I'll discharge."

"It's better, and does its work cleaner," grumbled the man sullenly ; and he gave his superior a morose look from under his shaggy brows.

"I don't care if it's a hundred times better. Go and blast the block down with powder, as it always has been done, I tell you again. I want my men; and there's no trusting that other stuff, or they're not fit to be trusted with it. Now go, and don't come here again without being summoned."

"Too grand for the likes o' me, eh, Master Gartram?"

"Will you have the goodness to recollect that you are speaking to a gentleman, sir?"

"I'm speaking to another man, I being a man," said Woodham sturdily. "I don't know nothing about no gentlemen. I'm speaking to Norman Gartram, quarry-owner, who lives here in riches and idleness upon what we poor slaves have made for him by the sweat of our brows."

"What does this mean?" cried the old man. "Have you turned Socialist?"

"I've turned nowt. But as a Christian man I warn you, Norman Gartram, that for all your fine house and your bags of money, and company and purple and fine linen, 'the Lord gave, and the Lord taketh away.'"

" You—"

" There, I'm going to do my work honest, master, and earn my wages."

" And blast that granite down with powder, sir."

" I know my work," grumbled the man, and he backed out of the room without another word.

Norman Gartram—the King of the Castle, as he was called at Danmouth—stood listening to the man's footsteps, at first heavy and dull as they passed over the carpet, and then loud and echoing as he reached the granite paving outside, till they died away, and then, with his face still flushed, he laid his hand gently on his temples.

" A little hot," he muttered. " A fit? Enough to give any man a fit to be spoken to like that by the canting scum. They're spoiled, that's what it is—spoiled. Claude is always fooling and petting them, and the more there is done for them the worse they work, and the more exacting they grow. I believe they think one's capital is to be sunk solely to benefit them. What the deuce do you want now ?"

This to the servant, who had timidly opened the door.

"I beg your pardon, sir."

"If it's some one from the quarry, tell him I'm engaged."

"Mr Glyddyr, sir."

"Why didn't you say so before? Where is he?"

"In the drawing-room, sir."

Norman Gartram sprung at once from his chair, hurriedly crossed the room, stepped out of the window on to the granite paving, which did duty in his garden for a gravel walk, carefully closed the French casement, and locked it with a small pass-key he carried in his pocket, and walked round to the verandah in front of the house, entering by the French window of the drawing-room, where a tall, handsome man of about thirty was leaning against a table, apparently admiring the brown leather shoes which formed part of his yachting costume.

"Ah, Mr Glyddyr, glad to see you. Kept your word, then?"

"Oh, yes; I always do that," said the

visitor, shaking hands warmly. "Not come at an inconvenient time, have I—not too busy?"

"Never too busy to receive friends," said Gartram. "Sit down, sit down."

"Miss Gartram none the worse for her visit to the yacht?"

"Oh, by no means; enjoyed it thoroughly."

"I could see that little Miss Dillon did, but I thought Miss Gartram seemed rather bored."

"Oh dear, no; nothing of the kind; but you'll have something?"

"Eh? No, thanks. Too early."

"A cigar?"

"Cigar? Oh, come, I can't refuse that."

"Come into my room, then. Obliged to obey the female tyranny of my household, Mr Glyddyr. I'm supposed to be master, but woman rules, sir, woman rules. My daughter does what she pleases with me."

"Happy man!"

"Eh?"

"I say happy man, sir, to be ruled by such a queen."

Norman Gartram gave him a keen look.

" Don't pay compliments, sir—society compliments. We are out of all society. I've
kept my daughter out of it. Only a tradesman."

" Lord Gartram's brother a tradesman, sir ? "

" Yes ; why not ? Why shouldn't he be ?
My father left my brother and me with a few ·
hundred pounds a-piece, and the prestige of
being nobleman's sons, sir. I had to consider
what I should do—loaf about through draw-
ing-rooms as a beggarly aristocrat, always in
debt till I could cajole a rich girl into making
me her poodle ; or take off my coat and go to
work like a man. Be a contemptible hanger-
on, too poor to dress well, or a sturdy, hard-
working human being."

" And your choice, sir ? " said the visitor,
inquiring for what he knew by heart.

" The latter, sir. I bit my nails down to
the quick till I had an idea—sitting out on
this very coast. I was yonder smoking a
bad cigar which my brother had given me.
I couldn't afford to buy cigars, neither could
he, but he bought them all the same. I sat
smoking that cigar and thought out what I

was sitting upon—granite—and went back to the hotel where we were staying, and told my brother what I had thought out. He called me a fool, and went his way. I, being a fool, went mine."

"Yes, sir?"

"My brother," said Gartram, "married a shrewish, elderly woman with some money. I spent all I had in buying a few acres of the cliff land by the side of this coast. Brother Fred said I must be mad. Perhaps I am; but my cliff quarry has supplied granite for some of the finest buildings in England. It has made me a rich man, while my Lord Gartram has to ask his wife for every shilling he wants to spend—when he does not ask me. But here, come along; I never know when to stop if I begin talking about myself. This way."

He led the visitor into his study, unlocked an oaken door in the wall with a bright key, and it swung open heavily, showing that the oak covered a slab of granite, and that the closet was formed of the same glittering stone.

"Curious place to keep cigars, eh? All

granite, sir. I believe in granite. Take one
of these," he continued, as he carelessly placed
a couple of cedar boxes on the table. "Light
up. I'll have one too. Bad habit at this
time in the morning, but one can't be always
at work, eh ? "

"No, sir ; and you work too hard, if report
is correct."

"Hang report!" said the old man, taking
a cigar, throwing himself back in a chair,
and gazing at his visitor through his half-
closed eyes. "That a good one ? "

"Delicious!" said the visitor laconically,
and there was silence.

"What do you think of my place, eh ? "

"Solid. Quite stand a siege."

"I meant it to, sir. There isn't a spot
where I could use granite instead of wood
that it is not used. Granite arches instead of
beams everywhere. When I have my gate
locked at night, I can laugh at all the burglars
in Christendom."

"Yes ; I should think you are pretty safe
here."

There was another pause, broken by Gartram saying suddenly, in a loud, sharp voice,—

" Well ? "

The visitor was a cool man about town, but the query was so sudden and unexpected that he started.

" Well, Mr Gartram ? "

" Why did you come this morning ? "

" You asked me to look in—a friendly call."

" Won't do. If you had meant a friendly call you would have come in the afternoon. You don't want to borrow money ? "

" Good heavens, sir ! No."

" Then out with it, lad. You are not a boy now. I am an old man of the world; speak out frankly, and let's get it done."

" You guess the object of my visit, then, sir ? "

" No ; I can feel it. Besides, I'm not blind."

Parry Glyddyr looked at his host with a half-amused, half-vexed expression of countenance.

" No," he said thoughtfully, in reference to Gartram's last remark ; " I suppose not, sir. Well, it is an awkward thing to do, and I may as well get it over. I will be frank."

"Best way, sir, if you wish to get on with me."

Glyddyr cleared his throat, became deeply interested in the ash of his cigar, and lolled back in his easy chair, quite conscious of the fact that his host was scanning him intently.

"I can sail my yacht as well as the master, Mr Gartram; I have a good seat in the hunting field, and I don't funk my hedges; I am a dead shot; you know I can throw a fly; and I am not a bad judge of a horse; but over a talk like this I am a mere faltering boy."

"Glad to hear it, sir, and hope it is your first essay.   Go on."

"Well, I came here nine months ago to repair damages after a storm, and you did me several pleasant little services."

"Never mind them."

"I came again at the end of another three months in fine weather."   .

"And you have been here several times since.   Go on."

"Yes, sir," said Glyddyr, smiling; "but are all fathers like you?"

"No," said Gartram, with a hoarse laugh; "I am the only one of my kind. There, we have had enough preamble, Parry Glyddyr. Out with it."

"I will, sir. You say you are not blind. You know, then, that I was deeply impressed by Miss Gartram the first time we met. I treated it as a temporary fancy, but the feeling has grown upon me, till I can only think of doing one thing—coming to you as a gentleman, telling you frankly I love Miss Gartram, and asking your permission to visit here regularly as her accepted suitor."

"What does Claude say to this?"

"Miss Gartram?" said Glyddyr, raising his eyebrows, and removing the grey ash from the end of his cigar; "nothing, sir. How could I be other than the ordinary acquaintance without your sanction?"

"Quite right," said Gartram, looking at him searchingly, "how, indeed?" and he remained gazing at the unshrinking countenance before him, full of candour and surprise at his ignorance of etiquette till he covered his own eyes. "Then Claude knows nothing of this?"

"I hope and believe, sir, that she knows a great deal, but not from my lips. Women, I believe, are very quick in knowing when they are admired."

"Humph! And you like my daughter, Mr Glyddyr?" said Gartram, exhaling a huge cloud of smoke.

"I love Miss Gartram very dearly, sir," said the visitor frankly; "so well that I dare not even think of the consequence of a refusal."

"Broken heart, suicide and that sort of think, eh?"

"I hope I should never make a fool of myself, Mr Gartram," said Glyddyr coldly.

"So do I. Now look here, sir. I gave up society to become a business man — slave driver some people politely call me; but as a tradesman I have been so tricked and swindled by everybody, even my banker, that I have grown suspicious."

"I don't wonder, sir. Without going into trade, a man has to keep his eyes open to the rascality of the world."

"Yes," said Gartram, scanning the speaker

keenly still. "Then now, sir, let me ask you a question."

"By all means; as many as you like."

"Then pray, sir, if my daughter had been a penniless girl, would you have felt this deep admiration for her?"

"Mr Gartram!" said Glyddyr haughtily, as he flushed deeply and rose from his chair. "Bah!" he added, after a pause, and he let himself sink back, and smoked heavily for a few moments. "Stupid to be so put out. Quite a natural question. Really, sir," he said, smiling, and looking ingenuously in the old man's face, "fate has been so kind to me over money matters that fortune-hunting has not been one of my pursuits. In round numbers, my father left me three hundred thousand pounds. Golden armour, sir, against the arrow of poverty, and such as turns aside so fierce a stab as that of yours. Has Miss Gartram any money?"

"Humph! I have," said the old man roughly.

"If she has, so much the better," continued Glyddyr, smoking calmly, and evidently thoroughly enjoying his cigar. " A lady with a private purse of her own no doubt occupies a more happy and independent position than one who appeals to her husband for all she wants. I am sorry that our conversation has taken this turn, Mr Gartram," he added stiffly.

" I'm not, Glyddyr. It has shown you up in another light. Well, what do you want me to say ? "

" To say, sir ? " cried the young man eagerly.

" Yes. There, I don't think I need say anything. Yes, I do. I don't like the idea of Claude marrying any one, but nature is nature. I shall be carried off some day by a fit, I suppose, and when I am, I believe—slave driver as I am, and oppressor of the poor, as they call me, for making Danmouth a prosperous place, and paying thousands a year in wages—I should rest more comfortably if I knew my child was married to the man she loved."

" Mr Gartram."

" I haven't done, Glyddyr,"

There was a pause, during which the old

man seemed to look his visitor through and through. Then he held out his hand with a quick, sharp movement.

"Yes," he said; "I like you, my lad: I always did. You think too much of sport; but you'll weary of that, and your whole thoughts will be of the best and truest girl that ever lived."

"Then you consent, Mr Gartram?" cried Glyddyr with animation.

"No: I consent to nothing. You've got to win her first. I give you my leave, though, to win if you can; and if you do marry her—well, I daresay I can afford to buy her outfit —trousseau—what you may call it."

"Mr Gartram—"

"That will do. Be cool. You haven't won her yet, my lad."

"I may speak to her at once?"

"If you like; but my advice is—don't. Lead up to it gently—make sure of her before you speak. There, I'm a busy man, and I've got to go up the east river to look at a vein of stone which crops up there. Take another cigar, and walk with me—if you like."

" I will, sir. Try one of mine."

" Yes," said Gartram laconically ; and as they went out into the hall, he purposely picked out his worst hat from the stand, and put it on.

" Old chap wants to make me shy at him, and show that I don't like walking through the town with that hat. Got hold of the wrong pig by the ear," said Glyddyr to himself.

They walked along the granite terrace, with its crenellated parapet and row of imitation guns, laboriously chipped out of the granite ; and then out through the gateway and over the moat, and descended to the village, reaching the path leading to the east glen, and were soon walking beside the rushing salmon river, with Gartram pointing out great veins of good granite as it cropped out of the side of the deep ravine.

" Hang his confounded stone !" said Glyddyr to himself, after he had made several attempts to change the drift of the conversation.

" Fine bit of stuff that, sir," said his companion, pointing across the river with his

heavy stick. " I believe I could cut a mono-
lith twenty feet long out of that rock, but the
brutes won't let me have it. My solicitor has
fought for it hard, but they stick to it, and
money won't tempt them. I believe that was
the beginning of my sleeplessness—insomnia,
as Asher calls it."

" Asher ? "

" Yes ; our doctor. You must know him.
Pleasant, smooth-spoken fellow in black."

" Oh, yes ; of course."

" Worried me a deal, that did."

" And you suffer from insomnia ? "

" Horribly. Keep something to exorcise
the demon, though," he said laughingly,
taking a small bottle from his pocket.
" Chloral."

" Dangerous stuff, sir. Take it cautiously."

" I take it as my medical man advises."

" That is right. Of course I remember
Doctor Asher, and that other young friend of
yours—the naturalist and salmon fisherman,
and—"

" Oh, Lisle. Yes ; sort of ward of mine.
I am his trustee."

"Quite an old friend, then, sir?"

"Yes; and—eh?" said the old man laughingly. "Why, Glyddyr, I can read you like a book. Is there, or has there ever been, anything between Claude and Christopher Lisle? I should think not, indeed. Rubbish, man, rubbish! and—"

They had just turned one of the rugged corners of the glen, and there before them in the distance was Chris Lisle helping Claude to catch a fish—his words, of course, inaudible, but his actions sufficiently demonstrative to make Parry Glyddyr press his teeth hardly together, and the owner of the granite castle grip his stick and swear.

CHAPTER III.

LESSON THE FIRST.

THINGS that seem far-fetched are sometimes simple matters of fact. Just as Claude was glancing back, and feeling as if she would give anything to be back home, a dove among the trees in the fern-clad glen began to coo, and Mary laughed.

"There," she said, "only listen. You can't go back now. It would be absurd."

"But you are so imprudent," whispered Claude, whose cheeks were growing hotter. "How could you?"

"I wanted to see you happy, my darling coz," was whispered back. "I saw him coming here with his fishing-rod, and—"

"But, Mary, what will Chris Lisle think?"

"Think he's in luck, and bless poor little humpy, fairy godmother me, and—no, no, too late to retreat. We have been seen."

For as they had passed out into an open part of the glen where the river widened into a pool, there, only a short distance from them, and with his bright, sun-browned face directed toward the river, was a sturdy, well-built young fellow, dressed in a dark tweed Norfolk jacket and knickerbockers, busily throwing a fly across the pool till, as if intuitively becoming aware that he was watched, he looked sharply round.

The next moment there was again the peculiar buzzing sound made by a rapidly-wound-up multiplying winch, the rod was thrown over the young man's shoulder, and he turned to meet them.

" Ah, little Mary ! " he cried merrily ; and then, with a voice full of tender reverence, he turned, straw hat in hand, to Claude.

" I did not expect to see you here."

" And I am as much surprised," she said hastily. " Mary and I were having a walk."

" And now we are here, Mr Lisle, you may as well show us all your salmon," said Mary seriously.

" My salmon ! I haven't had a rise."

" And we have interrupted you, perhaps, just as the fish are biting. Come, Mary. Good-morning, Mr Lisle."

" Oh ! "

Only a little interjection, but so full of reproach that Claude coloured here deeply, and more deeply still as, upon looking round for her companion, she found her comfortably seated upon a mossy stone, and with her head turned away to hide the mischievous delight which flashed from her eyes.

" I'm beginning to be afraid that I have offended you, Miss Gartram—Claude."

" Oh, no ; what nonsense. Come, Mary."

The stone upon which she sat was not more deaf.

" Don't hurry away. I thought I was some day to give you a lesson in salmon fishing."

" I should never learn, Mr Lisle ; and, besides, it is not a very ladylike accomplishment."

" Anything you did, Claude, would be ladylike. Come, I know there are two or three salmon in this pool. They will not rise for me ; they might for you."

" I should scare them away."

" No," said the young man meaningly ;
" you would attract anything to stay."

" Mr Lisle ! "

" Well, what have I said ? There, forgive
me, and take the rod. You promised I should
show you how to throw a fly."

" Yes, yes ; but some other time—perhaps
to-morrow."

" To-morrow comes never," said the young
man laughingly. " No ; I have my chance
now. Miss Dillon, did not your cousin
promise to let me show her how to catch
a salmon ? "

" Yes ; and I am so tired. I'll wait till you
have caught one, Claude."

" There," cried the young man hurriedly ;
and the stronger will prevailing over the
weaker, Claude allowed her instructor to
thrust the lithe rod he held into her hands,
and, trembling and blushing, she suffered herself to be led to the side of the pool.

" I shall never learn," she said.

" Not learn ! I shall be able to come up
to the Fort carrying your first salmon, and

to say to Mr Gartram : 'There, sir ; salmon fishing taught in one lesson.' What do you say to that ? "

" How can she be so foolish ?—Of what am I talking ?—Mr Lisle, pray let me go."

All silent sentences, but as the last was thought Claude raised her eyes to her companion, to meet his fixed upon hers, so full of tender, reverent love that she dropped her own, and fell a-trembling with a joy she tried vainly to crush down, while her heart beat heavily the old, old theme,—

" He loves me well—he loves me well."

They had known each other since they were boy and girl, and the affection had slowly and steadily grown stronger and stronger, but Chris Lisle had said to himself time after time that it was too soon to tell her his love, and ask for the guardianship of her heart ; and he had waited, feeling satisfied that some day Claude Gartram would be his.

" There," he said playfully, " now for lesson the first. Let me draw out some more line. That's the way. Now, you know as well as I do how to throw. Try to let your fly fall amongst that foam below where the water rushes into the pool. That's the way. Bravo ! "

" There, Mr Lisle," cried Claude, after making a very fair cast, " now take the rod, for I must go. Mary, dear, come along."

" Sha'n't," said Mary to herself, as she grew more deaf than ever. " Gather your rosebuds while you may, dear. He's a nice, good fellow. Ah ! how I could have loved a man like that."

" Mary Dillon is too much interested in her book," said Chris. " There, that's plenty of line for a good cast. You must go on now. It isn't so very wicked, Claude."

" There, then, this one throw and I must go," said the girl, her cheeks burning, and her head seeming to swim, for she was conscious of nothing—running river, the foam and swirl, the glorious landscape of rugged glen side, and the bright sun gilding the heathery earth upon which she stood—conscious of nothing save the fact that Chris Lisle was by her, and that his words seemed to thrill her to the heart, while in spite of herself he seemed to have acquired a mastery over her which it was sweet to obey.

"Well back," he cried ; "now then, a good one."

It was not a good cast, being a very clumsy one, for the fly fell with a splash right out in a smooth, oily looking patch of water behind some stones. But, as is often the case, the tyro is more successful than the tried fisherman. The fly had no sooner touched the water than there was a rise, a singing whirr from the winch, and Chris shouted aloud with joy.

"There !" he cried. "You have him. First lesson."

"Have I caught it ?"

"Yes, yes ; hold up the point of your rod."

Claude immediately held it down, and the line went singing out, till Chris darted close behind his pupil and seized the rod, just over her hands, raising the top till it bent nearly double.

"A beauty !" he cried excitedly. "You lucky girl !"

"Thank you. That's right. Now, take the rod and pull it out."

"No, no," he said, with his lips close to her ear, and she trembled more and more as she felt his crisp beard tickle the back of her neck, and his strong arms tightly press hers to her sides; "you must land him now."

Away darted the salmon wildly about the pool, but Claude could not tell whether it was the excitement caused by the electric messages sent through the line, or by the pressure of Chris Lisle's hands as he held hers to the rod.

"Mary, come and see Mr Lisle catch this salmon," she cried huskily; but Mary only turned over a leaf, and seemed more deaf than ever, while the fish tugged and strained.

"Mr Lisle, loose my hands now. This is absurd. What are you doing?'

"Telling you I love you," he whispered, in spite of himself, for the time had come, "Claude, dearest, better than my life."

"No, no; you must not tell me that," she said, half tearfully, for the declaration seemed to give her pain.

"I must. The words have come at last."

"And you have lost your fish," cried Claude, for the line had suddenly become slack.

"But have I won you?"

"No, no. And pray let me go now."

"No?"

There was so much anguish in the tone in which that one little word was spoken, that it went right to Claude's heart, and as if involuntarily, she added quickly,—

"I don't know."

"Claude, dearest," he whispered, and his voice trembled as the words were breathed in her ear, "for pity's sake don't trifle with me."

"I am not trifling with you. I told you the truth. I don't know."

"Ah, that's not catching salmon," came sharply from behind them. "Claude, dear, don't listen to him. He's a wicked fortune-hunter."

Chris started away from Claude as if some one had struck him a violent blow.

"Mary!" cried Claude.

"Oh, I beg your pardon. What did I say?"
Whizz!

"Mr Lisle! Help!" cried Claude, for the

line had suddenly tightened, the top of the rod bent over in a curve, and the winch sang out as it rapidly revolved.

"Take the rod, please, Mr Lisle," continued Claude, in a voice full of emotion; and, as he took it without a word, she saw that he was deadly pale, and that his white teeth were pressing hard upon his nether lip.

He played the fish mechanically, and with Claude steadily looking on, and feeling as if she would like to run home to shut herself in her own room and throw herself upon her knees and sob. But the face before her held her as by a chain, and she turned with a bitter look of reproach upon her cousin, as she saw the way in which Chris was stung.

"Don't look at me like that, dear," cried Mary, "the words slipped out. I did not mean them, indeed. It's a big fish, isn't it, Mr Lisle? Shall I gaff it for you?"

"Thank you," he said drearily; and Mary picked up the bamboo staff with the glistening hook at the end.

"Oh, I do beg your pardon, Mr Lisle."

"Granted," was the laconic reply.

"Don't, pray, don't punish me for saying those words," cried Mary. "There, finish your lesson in love and fishing. Claude," she whispered, as the young man had to follow the fish a few yards down the stream, "you've caught him tightly; shall I gaff him as well?"

"Yes; you had better finish your lesson, Miss Gartram," said Chris, walking back slowly winding in the line, and speaking in a hard, cold tone.

"No; you had better finish," she replied hastily; and then, as she saw the cloud deepening on his brow, she stepped forward quickly, and laid her hand on the rod. "Yes, let me finish, Chris," she said, and she gazed at him with her eyes full of faith and trust.

"Claude," he whispered, as he gave her the rod, "you couldn't think—"

"Hallo! What's this?" cried a harsh voice, and all started, so suddenly had Norman Gartram—followed closely by his visitor —stepped up to where they stood.

"Mr Lisle giving Claude and me a lesson in fishing," said Mary sharply. "Now, Claude, dear, wind in and I'll hook him out."

"Most interesting group," said Parry Glyddyr, with rather a contemptuous look at the teacher of the art.

"Very," said Norman Gartram, frowning. "Here, Claude, stop that fooling and come home."

"Mary, Mary, what have you done?" whispered Claude, as they walked away.

"Made a mess of it, darling, I'm afraid."

As they turned a corner of the glen, with her father's guest talking about what she did not know, Claude stole a glance back, to see Christopher Lisle standing with his hands resting upon the rod he held, and a bright, silvery fish lying at his feet.

The girl's heart went on beating heavily with pulsations that seemed as full of pleasure as of pain.

CHAPTER IV.

"ALL TO BITS!"

MARY DILLON did the greater part of the talking on the way home, Gartram saying scarcely a word, but making great use of his eyes, to see how Glyddyr took the unpleasant *contretemps*.

"And just after what I had said to him," muttered Gartram. "The insolent young scoundrel! The miserable, contemptible pauper! How dare he?"

But Glyddyr's behaviour was perfect, and excited Gartram's wonder.

"He can't have seen what I did," he thought, "or he would never talk to her so coolly."

For, ignoring everything, and as if he was blind to what had passed, Glyddyr dashed at once into a series of inquiries about Danmouth, and the weather in the winter.

"Do the storms affect the place much?" he said, looking at Claude.

" Knock the pots off sometimes, and always wash the slates clean," said Mary, before Claude could reply.

"Not pleasant for the inhabitants," said Glyddyr, after giving Mary a quick, amused glance before turning again to Claude. "But at the Fort, of course, you are too high up for the waves to reach?"

"Salt spray coats all the windows, and makes the walls shine," interposed Mary.

"What will he think of me?" thought Claude; and then she wondered that she did not feel sorry, but that all the time, in spite of her father's fiercely sullen looks, a peculiar kind of joy seemed to pervade her breast.

Glyddyr talked on, but he was completely talked down by Mary, who felt that the kindest thing she could do was to draw every one's attention from her cousin, till they had passed through the little town, and nearly reached the Fort, where they were met by a rough-looking workman, who ran unceremoniously towards them, caught hold of Gartram roughly, and cried out, in wild excitement,—

" Come on to the quarry at once."

"What's the matter—fall of rock?" cried Gartram.

"Blasting—Woodham—blown all to bits," panted the man.

"Then he has been using dynamite."

"Nay; soon as we picked him up, he said it was the cursed bad powder."

"Bah! Where is he?"

"We took him home, and I fetched the doctor, and then come on here."

"Run home, girls. No, Mr Glyddyr, see them in. I'm going on to my workmen's cottages."

He hurried off, and Glyddyr turned to Claude.

"I'm sorry there is such terrible news," he began; but Claude did not seem to hear him.

"Make haste, Mary," she said hurriedly. "Bring brandy and wine, and join me there."

"My dear Miss Gartram, are you going to the scene of the accident?"

Claude looked at him in an absent way.

"I am going to the Woodhams' cottage,"

she said hurriedly. "Sarah Woodham was our old servant. Don't stop me, please."

She hurried along the narrow road leading west, and it was not until she had gone some hundred yards following the messenger, who was trotting heavily at Gartram's heels, that she realised that she was not alone.

"Mr Glyddyr!" she exclaimed.

"Pray pardon me," he said, in a low, earnest voice. "As a friend, I cannot let you go alone at a time like this."

Claude looked up at him wildly, but there was so much respectful deference in his manner that she could say nothing. In fact, her thoughts were all with the suffering man and woman—the victims of this deplorable mishap.

It was nearly half-a-mile along the rough cliff road; and it was traversed in silence, Claude being too much agitated to say more.

The scene was easy enough to find when they were approaching the place, for a knot of rough quarry workmen were gathered round a clean-looking, white-washed cottage, from out of whose open door came the harsh tones of a

man's voice, while the crowd parted left and
right, and several placed the short black pipes
they were smoking hurriedly in their pockets.

Claude had nearly reached the door when
the words which were being uttered within
the cottage seemed to act like a spell, arrest-
ing her steps and making her half turn
shuddering away, as they seemed to lash her,
so keenly and cuttingly they fell.

"Curse you! curse you! It's all your doing.
You've murdered me. Sarah, my girl, he has
done for me at last."

Gartram's voice was heard in low, deep,
muttering tones, as if in reproof; but the
injured man's voice overbore it directly,
sounding shrill and harsh from agony as he
cried,—

"Let every one outside hear it. Hark ye,
lads, I wanted to use the dinnymite, but he
made me use the cursed old powder again, and
he has murdered me."

"My good man," said a fresh voice, which
sounded clear in the silence, "you must be
calm. It was a terrible accident."

"Nay, doctor, it's his doing; it's his meanness. I wanted him to use the dinnymite, and he would keep to powder. He has murdered me."

There was a low groan, and then a terrible cry; and as Glyddyr mentally pictured the scene within, of the doctor dressing the injuries, he turned to the trembling girl beside him.

"Miss Gartram," he whispered, "this is no place for you. There is plenty of help. Let me see you home."

She shook her head as she looked at him wildly, and, making a deprecating gesture, Glyddyr turned to one of the men.

"Is he very bad?" he whispered.

"Blowed a'most to bits," said the man in a hoarse whisper.

"Did the powder go off too soon?"

"It warn't powder at all," said the man, as Gartram stepped quickly out of the cottage. "It were the dinnymite. He would use it, and he warn't used to its ways."

It was evident from the peculiar tightening of Gartram's lips that he had heard the man's words; and he turned back and re-entered the cottage, for his name was sharply pronounced within.

Then there was another groan, and the injured man cried,—

"Don't, don't; you're killing me."

At that moment a thin, keen - looking woman of about thirty rushed out of the cottage, her eyes wild and staring, and her face blanched, while her hands and apron were horribly stained.

"I can't bear it," she cried; "I can't bear it!" and she flung herself upon her knees in the stony road, and covered her face with her hands, sobbing hysterically.

The sight of the suffering woman roused Claude to action; and as she took a couple of steps forward, and with the tears falling fast, laid her hand upon the woman's shoulder, a low murmur arose among the men, and Glyddyr saw that they drew back respectfully, several turning right away.

"Sarah, my poor Sarah," said Claude, bending low.

At the tender words of sympathy and the touch of the gentle hands, the woman let her own fall from her face, and stared up appealingly at the speaker.

Claude involuntarily shrank away from the ghastly face, for the hands had printed hideous traces upon the woman's brow.

The shrinking away was momentary, for, recovering herself, Claude drew her handkerchief from her pocket, to turn in surprise as it was drawn from her hand, but she directly gave Glyddyr a grateful look, as she saw him step to a rough granite trough into which a jet of pure water was pouring from the cliff, and saturating it quickly, he returned the handkerchief to its owner.

But before the blood stains could be removed, the voice of the injured man was heard calling.

"Sarah! Don't leave me, my girl. He has murdered me."

The woman gave Claude a wild look, rose from her knees, and tottered back to the cottage as the voice of Gartram was heard in angry retort.

"It's like talking to a madman, Ike Woodham," came clear and loud; "but you've got hurt by your own wilful obstinacy, and you want to throw the blame on me."

As he spoke, Gartram strode out of the cottage, and then whispered to his child,—

"Come home, my dear. You can do no good."

"No, no; not yet, papa," she whispered. "I must try if I can help poor Sarah in her terrible trouble."

A low murmur arose from the little crowd, and this seemed to excite Gartram.

"Well," he cried fiercely, "what does that mean? It was his own fault—in direct opposition to my orders; and this is not the first accident through your own folly."

The low, angry muttering continued.

"Here, come away, Claude," cried Gartram fiercely, as he looked round at the lowering faces.

"He has murdered me, I tell you!" came from the open cottage door.

"Bah!" ejaculated Gartram angrily, and he strode away, but returned directly.

"Are you coming, my girl?"

"Yes, papa, soon. Let me see if I can be of use."

"Look here, Mr Glyddyr," said Gartram, speaking in a low, excited voice, "I can't stop. I shall be saying things that will make them mad. See after Claude, and bring her home. The senseless idiots! If a man bruises himself with his own hammer, it is blamed on me."

He strode away, and ignoring Glyddyr's presence, Claude was moving softly toward the door, when the man who had brought the message held out his hand to arrest her.

"Don't go in, dear bairn," he said in a husky whisper; "it isn't for the likes of you to see."

"Thank you, Wolfe," she said calmly, "I am not afraid."

But at that moment, as Glyddyr was about to make a protest, a quiet-looking, gentlemanly man appeared at the door turning down his cuffs, the perspiration glistening upon his high white forehead as he came out into the sun.

"No, no, my dear child," he said in a whisper, as a low moaning came from within and seemed to be followed by the low soft washing of the waves below. "You can do no good."

"Is—is he very bad, Doctor Asher?" asked Claude.

He looked at her for an instant or two with
out replying, and then bent his head.

"Oh !" ejaculated Claude, with a low cry of
pain.

"Terribly crushed, my dear; better leave
them together alone."

"But — you do not think — oh, Doctor
Asher, you can save him?"

"Is it so bad as that, sir?" whispered
Glyddyr, as he saw the peculiar look in the
doctor's face. "Couldn't you—with more
help—shall I send?"

"My dear sir," said the doctor in a low
voice, "half a dozen of the crack London
surgeons couldn't save him."

"Oh !" sighed Claude again. "But a
clergyman. Mr Glyddyr, would you go into
Danmouth?"

"Better not, my dear child," said the doctor
quietly. "You know their peculiar tenets.
His wife was praying with him when I came
out."

As if to endorse the doctor's words, the low,
constant murmur of a voice was heard from
within, and from time to time a gasping utter-

ance was heard, and then twice over the word
" Amen."

Just then Claude stepped softly toward the
open doorway, and sank upon her knees with
her hands clasped, and her face turned up appealingly toward the sunny sky, while all
around seemed full of life and hope, though
the black shadow of death was closing in upon
the humble roof. And as Glyddyr saw the
sweet, pure, upturned face, with its closed
eyes, he involuntarily took off his hat, and
gazed wistfully, with something very near akin
to love seeming to swell within his breast.

The silence was very deep, though the
murmur from the cottage continued, till, in
the midst of what seemed to be a painful
pause, a loud and bitter wail came upon the
stillness, and the doctor hurriedly stepped
within.

"Poor Ike's cottage is to let, mates," said
a rough, low voice; "who wants to make a
change ? "

"Dead ? " asked Claude, with a motion of
her lips, as after a short space the doctor
returned.

"No; the draught I have given him to dull the pain has had effect : he is asleep."

"And when he awakes, Doctor Asher?" whispered Claude, as she clung to his arm.

The doctor shook his head.

"Can you do nothing?"

"Only try to lull the pain," was the reply. And then quickly, "Wanted somewhere else?"

This last was to himself as a man was seen running toward them, and Claude turned if possible paler as she recognised one of the servants from the Fort.

He ran up breathlessly.

"Miss Claude—Doctor Asher," he panted. "Come at once. Master's got another of his fits."

"Don't be flurried, my dear," said Doctor Asher, as, in a calm, business-like way, he saw to Gartram being laid easily on the floor, where he had fallen in the study.

"But he looks so ghastly. You do not think—"

"Yes, I do, my child," said the doctor cheerfully. "Not what you think, because I know. He has another fit precisely the same as the last, and it was evidently a sudden seizure, just as he had risen from his chair, after writing that letter."

"Then there is no danger?"

"Oh, dear, no. That's right, you see. We'll have this mattress on the floor; and he can lie here. Don't be alarmed."

"But I am horribly alarmed."

"Then you must not be, my child. I will not conceal the fact from you that he will probably be subject to more fits, and may have one at any time."

"But I feel so helpless."

"So does a doctor, my dear. We try all we can, but time has to perform the greater part of the cure, after we have done all we can to avoid suffocation, and the patient injuring himself in his struggles. There, there; he's going on all right, and you've been a very good, brave girl. I quite admire your behaviour all through; and another time, if I am not here, you will know exactly how to act."

"Oh, don't talk of another time, Doctor Asher."

"Well, I will not," he said, smiling. "Now, don't be alarmed, but keep perfectly cool, for I must go back and see to that poor fellow at the quarry."

"Yes, of course. But, doctor, if my poor father should be taken worse?"

"He will not be taken worse, but gradually mend. I shall not be very long away."

"No, no; pray don't be long."

"No; and mind you are my assistant. So you must be cool and self-possessed. Shall I send Miss Dillon to sit with you?"

" Yes, please, do," said the agitated girl, as she gazed wildly at her father's altered face.

Doctor Asher seemed rather to resemble a very smooth, black tom cat, and, as he drew down his cuffs, and passed his white hands over his glossy coat, an imaginative person would not have been much surprised to see him begin to lick himself, to remove a few specks caused by the business in which he had been engaged.

As he left the study and crossed the hall, with its polished granite flooring, his delicate manner of proceeding toward the drawing-room, and stepping from one to another of the oases of Eastern rugs, was still like the progress of the cat who believed the polished granite to be water, and tried to avoid wetting his paws.

When he laid his hand upon the drawing-room door, a murmur of voices came from within, and, as he entered, Mary Dillon jumped up from the low ottoman upon which she had been seated, talking to Glyddyr, and ran quickly to the doctor's side.

" How is he ? " she said excitedly.

"Better, certainly. Miss Gartram wants you to go and stay with her."

"Yes, of course. Good-bye, Mr Glyddyr, and thank you for being so kind."

She spoke as she ran to the door, jerked the last words back over her shoulder, and was gone, leaving the doctor face to face with the visitor.

"How is he?" said the latter. "You can speak plainly to me."

"To be sure I can, my dear sir. Ah, what a world this is. Yesterday we were taking our champagne in the saloon of your charming yacht, to-day—"

"You are keeping me waiting for an answer," said Glyddyr, rather stiffly.

"So I am," said the doctor, smiling. "Well, how is he? Rather bad. Nasty fit of his usual sort."

"Then he is subject to these fits?"

"Most decidedly."

"But what caused it?"

"Worry. From what I can gather, he must have some upset when out walking. Our friend has a temper."

"Ah!" ejaculated Glyddyr.

"Then he has had some quarrel with this poor fellow who is hurt. The terrible accident followed, and, with the customary crass obstinacy of rustic, ignorant workmen, the poor fellow and his comrades lay the blame of a trouble, caused by their own stupidity, upon their employer.

"Yes, I see. Caused great mental disturbance?"

"Exactly, my dear sir. He being a man who, in the labour of making money, has nearly worried himself to death."

"Yes."

"And who now worries himself far more to keep it."

"Ah, money is hard to keep," said Glyddyr, with a smile.

"He has found it so, sir. When the old bank broke years ago, it hit him to the tune of many thousands."

"Indeed!"

"Yes; and that set him building this place for his protection. I shouldn't wonder if he has quite a bank here."

" Indeed !   Then the old man is rich ? "

" Rich !   I thought every one knew that. Better be poor and happy."

" As we are, eh, doctor ?   Well, it's a terrible worry—money."

This was accompanied by a peculiar look which the doctor interpreted, and replied to with one as suggestive.

" No danger, I hope, to the old gentleman?"

" No, no.   Fits are not favourable to health, though.

" Well, no danger this time, I hope ? "

" Not a bit.   He'll feel the shock for a few days.   That's all."

" And the other patient ? "

" Hah, yes ; I'm just going over there."

" He is very bad, you say ? "

" Bad !   I expect to find him gone."

The doctor nodded, and left the room.

" Bah ! how I do hate them," said Glyddyr. " I'd have walked down with him, but I always feel as if I were smelling physic."

Glyddyr stood tapping the bottom of his watch, which he had just taken from his pocket, as he talked in a low tone, just as if he were conversing with the little round face before him.

"How wild the old boy was—just after he had been talking to me as he had. Pshaw! I don't mind. Rustic bit of courtship. Half-bumpkin sort of fellow, and poor as Job. Old man wouldn't have him at any price. The gipsy! Been carrying on with him, then, eh? Well, it's always the way with your smooth, drooping little violets. Regular flirtation. I don't mind. I wouldn't give a dump for a girl without a bit of spirit in her. It's all right. Friends at court — a big friend at court. But no more fits for friends—at present, I hope. I'll get him to come on a cruise, and bring her. Tell the old boy it will do him good. Get the doctor on my side, and make him prescribe a trip round the islands, with him to come as medical attendant. Nothing to do, and unlimited champagne. Real diplomacy. By Jupiter, Parry, you are a clever one, though you do get most awfully done on the turf!"

"Yes," he said, after another look at the watch, for the purpose now of seeing the time,

"that's the plan—a long sea trip round the
islands, with sentiment, sighs and sunsets;
and, as they said in the old melodramas,
'Once aboard the lugger, she is mine.' For,
lugger read steam yacht, schooner-rigged *Fair
Star*, of Cowes; Parry Glyddyr, owner."

He laughed in a low, self-satisfied way, and
then moved toward the door.

" Well, it's of no use to wait here," he said.
"They will not show up again. I can call,
though, as often as I like. Come again this
evening, and see her then. She can't refuse.
I'll go now and see how the salmon fisher is
getting on."

CHAPTER VI.

IN CHARGE.

"Mary, dear, don't deceive me for the sake of trying to give me comfort," said Claude, as she knelt in the study, beside the mattress upon which her father lay breathing stertorously.

"Claude, darling, I tease you and say spiteful things sometimes, but you know you can trust me."

"Yes, yes, dear, I know; but you don't answer me."

"I have told you again and again that your father is just like he was last time, and the best proof of there being no danger is Doctor Asher staying away so long."

"It's that which worries me so. He promised to come back soon."

"Don't be unreasonable, dear. You know he went to the quarry where that man is dangerously hurt."

"Yes. Poor Sarah! How she must suffer! It is very terrible. But look now, Mary— that dark mark beneath papa's eyes."

"Yes, I can see it," said Mary, rising quickly, and going to the table, where she changed the position of the lamp, with the result that the dark shadow lay now across the sleeper's lips. "There, that is not a dangerous symptom, Claudie."

"Don't laugh at me, Mary. You can't think how alarmed I am. These fits seem to come more frequently than they used. Ought not papa to have more advice?"

"It would be of no use, dear. I could cure him."

"You?"

"Yes; or he could cure himself."

"Mary!"

"Yes," said the little, keen-looking body, kneeling down by her cousin's side; "uncle has only to leave off worrying about making more money and piling up riches that he will never enjoy, and he would soon be well again."

Claude sighed.

"See what a life he leads, always in such a

hurry that he cannot finish a meal properly; and as to taking a bit of pleasure in any form, he would think it wicked. I haven't patience with him. Yes, I have, poor old fellow—plenty. He has been very good to miserable little me."

"Of course he has, dear," said Claude, throwing her arms about her cousin's neck and kissing her, with the result that the sharp-looking, self-contained little body uttered an hysterical cry, clung to her, and burst out sobbing wildly, as if all control was gone.

"Mary, darling, don't, pray don't. You distress me. What is the matter?"

"I'm miserable, wretched," sobbed the poor girl, with her face hidden in her cousin's breast. "I always seem to be doing something wrong. It's just as if, when I tried to make people happy, I was a kind of imp of mischief, and caused trouble."

"No, no, no! What folly."

"It isn't folly; it's quite true. See what I did this morning."

Claude felt her cheeks begin to burn, and she tried to speak, but the words would not come.

"I knew that Chris Lisle had gone up the east river fishing, and I was sure he longed to see you, and I was quite certain you wanted to see him."

"Mary, be silent," cried Claude, in an excited whisper; "it is not true."

"Yes, it is, dear. You know it is, and I could see that he was miserable, and had been since you went on board Mr Glyddyr's yacht, so I felt that it would be quite right to take you round there, so that you might meet and make it up. And see what mischief I seem to have made."

"Yes," said Claude gravely, as she metaphorically put on her maiden mask of prudery; "and you know now that it was very, very thoughtless of you."

"Thoughtless!" said Mary, looking up with a quick look, half-troubled, half-amused; "didn't I think too much?"

"Don't talk, Mary," said Claude primly. "You may disturb poor papa. It was very wicked and meddlesome and weak, and you don't know what harm you have done."

Mary Dillon's face was flushed and tear-stained, and her eyes looked red and troubled ; but she darted a glance at her cousin so full of mischievous drollery, that Claude's colour deepened, and she turned away troubled, and totally unable to continue the strain of reproof.

She was spared further trouble by a cough heard in the hall.

"Wipe your eyes quickly, Mary," she whispered ; "here is Doctor Asher at last."

Mary jumped up, and stepped to the window, where she was half hidden by the curtains, as there was a gentle tap at the door, the handle was turned, and the doctor, looking darker and more stern than ever, entered the room.

He whisperingly asked how his patient had been, as he went down on one knee by the mattress, made a short examination, and turned to Claude, who, with parted lips, was watching him anxiously.

"You think him worse ? " she whispered.

"Indeed I do not," he said quickly. "Nothing could be better. He will sleep heavily for a long time."

"But did you notice his heavy breathing ? "

"Of course I did," said the doctor rising,

"and you have no cause for alarm. Ah, Miss Mary, I did not see you at first."

"Don't deceive me, Doctor Asher," said Claude, in agonised tones; "tell me the worst."

"There is no worse to tell you, my dear child. I dare say your father will be well enough to sit up to-morrow."

"Thank heaven!" said Claude to herself. Then, turning to the doctor: "How is poor Isaac Woodham?"

"Don't ask me."

"How dreadful!"

"Yes; it was a terrible accident."

"But is there no hope?"

"You asked me not to deceive you," said the doctor gravely. "None at all."

Just then the sick man moaned slightly in his sleep, and made an uneasy movement which took his daughter back to his side.

"Don't be alarmed, my child," said the doctor encouragingly; "there is nothing to fear."

"But I am alarmed," said Claude; "and I look forward with horror to the long night when I am alone with him."

"You are going to sit up with him?"

"Of course."

"Divide the night with your cousin."

"Yes—but—"

"Well—what is it?"

"Oh, Doctor Asher, don't leave him. Pray, pray, stay here."

"But I have to go and see that poor fellow twice during the night."

"I had forgotten him," sighed Claude. "Couldn't you stop here, and go and see him in the night?"

"Well, I might do that," said the doctor thoughtfully; "but really, my child, there is no necessity."

"If you could stop, Doctor Asher," interposed Mary, "it would be a great relief to poor Claude, who is nervous and hysterical about my uncle's state."

"Very well," was the cheerful reply. "I'll tell you what; I'll sit with you till about nine, and then go and see poor Woodham. Then I'll come back and stay up with Mr Gartram till about three, when you shall be called to relieve me."

"But I shall not go to bed," said Claude decidedly.

"I am your medical man, and I prescribe rest," said the doctor, smiling. "I don't want any more patients at present. You and your cousin will go and lie down early, and then come and relieve me, so that I can go and see poor Woodham again. After that I shall return here, and you can let me have a sofa ready, to be called if wanted. There, I am the doctor, and a doctor rules in a sick house."

"Must I do as you say?" asked Claude pleadingly.

"Yes; you must," he replied; and so matters were settled.

Doctor Asher walked down to the quarry cottage to see his patient there, and did what he could to alleviate the poor fellow's pain, always avoiding the inquiring look in the wife's eyes, and then he returned to the Fort.

"How is he now?" asked Claude anxiously.

"Very bad," was the reply.

"You will find coffee all ready on the side-table, doctor," said Claude; "and there is a spirit lamp and the stand and glasses. There are cigars on the shelf; but you will let me sit up too?"

"To show that you have no confidence in your medical man."

"Oh, no, no; but Mary and I might be of some use."

"And of none at all to-morrow, my dears. You must both go to bed, and be ready to relieve me."

"But is there anything else I can do to help you?"

"Yes; what I say—go to bed at once."

Claude hesitated a few moments, and then walked quickly to the side of the mattress, knelt down, kissed her father lovingly, and then rose.

"Come, Mary," she said. "And you will ring the upstairs bell if there's the slightest need?"

"Of course, of course. There, good-night; I shall ring punctually at two."

He shook hands, and the two girls left the room unwillingly, and proceeded slowly upstairs.

"We'll lie down in your room, Mary," said

Claude; "it is so much nearer the bell. Do you know, I feel so dreadfully low-spirited? It is as if a terrible shadow had come over the place, and—don't laugh at me—it seemed to grow darker when Doctor Asher came into the room."

"What nonsense! Because he is all in black."

"Do you think he is to be trusted, Mary?"

"I don't know. I don't like him, and I never did. He is so sleek and smooth, and I hate him to call us 'my dear' in that nasty, patronising, paternal sort of way."

"Then let's sit up."

"No, no. It would be absurd. I daresay we should feel the same about any other doctor."

"I do hope he will take great care of poor papa," sighed Claude; and the door closed after them as they entered their room.

If Doctor Asher was not going to take great care of Norman Gartram, it was very evident that he was going to take very great care of himself, for as soon as he was alone he struck a match, lit the spirit lamp, lifted the lid of the coffee pot, and found that it was still very hot, and then, removing a stopper in the spirit stand, he poured out into a cup a goodly portion of pale brandy.

He had just restored the stopper to the spirit decanter, saying to himself, " Nice, thoughtful little girl !" when Gartram moaned and moved uneasily.

The doctor crossed to him directly, went down on one knee, and felt to see that his patient's neck was well opened.

" Almost a pity not to have had him undressed," he said to himself. " What's the matter with you—uncomfortable ? Why, poor old boy," he continued, with a half laugh, as his hands busily felt round the sick man, " how absurd ! "

He had passed a hand through the opening in Gartram's shirt front, and after a little effort succeeded in unbuckling a cash belt which was round his patient's waist, drawing the whole out, and noting that on one side there was a pocket stuffed full and hard as he threw the belt carelessly on the table.

" Nice wadge that for a man to lie on.

There, old fellow, you'll be more comfortable now."

As if to endorse his words, Gartram uttered a deep sigh, and seemed to settle off to sleep.

"Breeches pockets full too, I daresay," muttered the doctor; "and shouldn't be surprised if there's a good, hard bunch of keys somewhere in his coat. Doesn't trouble him, though."

He rose, and went back to the tray at the side, filled the already primed coffee cup and carried it to the table, wheeled forward an easy chair, selected a cigar, which he lit, and then threw himself back and sipped his coffee and smoked.

"Yes, sweet little girl Claude," he thought; "make a man a good wife—good rich wife, and if—no, no, not the slightest chance for me, and I'll go on as I am, and make the best of it."

He had another sip.

"Delicious coffee, fine cigar. Worse things than being a doctor. We get as much insight of family matters as the parsons, and are trusted with more secrets."

He laughed to himself as he lay back.

" Yes, nice little heiress, Claude," he said again. " Wonder who'll get her—Christopher the salmon fisher, or our new yachting friend ? I think I should back Glyddyr."

He smoked on, and thought seriously for some time about his other patient, and after a time he emitted a cloud of smoke which he had retained in his mouth, as he turned himself with a jerk from one side of his great easy chair to the other.

" No," he said, "impossible to have done more. The Royal College of Surgeons couldn't save him."

He smoked on in silence, sipping his coffee from time to time, gazing the while at Gartram, upon whom the light shone faintly, just sufficient to show his stern-looking, deeply-marked face.

" Yours is a good head, my dear patient," he mused. " Well-cut features, and a look of firm determination in your aspect, even when your eyes are closed. You miss something there, for you have keen, piercing eyes, but for all that you look like what you are, a stubborn, determined Englishman, who will have his own way

over everything so long as his works will make
him go. When they run down, he comes to
me for help, and I am helping him. Yes, you
were sure to get on and heap up money, and
build grand houses, and slap your pocket-book
and say : 'I am a rich man, and I laugh at
and deride the whole world,' and so you do, my
dear sir, all but the doctor, who, once he has
you, has you all his life, and can do what he
likes with you. I have you hard, Norman
Gartram, and I am licensed ; I have you completely under me, and so greatly am I in possession of you, that I could this night say to
you die, and you would die ; or I could bid
you live, and you would live. A simple giving
or a simple taking. A movement with the
tactus eruditus of a physician, and then the
flag would be down, the King of the Castle
would be gone, and a new king would reign
in the stead—or queen," he added, with a
laugh.

"Ah, you people trust us a great deal, and
we in return trust you—a very long time often
before we can get paid. Not you, my dear
Gartram, you always were a hard cash man.

But you people trust us a great deal, and our power is great.

"And ought not to be abused," he said hastily. "No, of course not. No one ought to abuse those who trust. Capital coffee this," he added, as he partook of more. "Grand thing to keep a man awake.

"Humph! Tired. Ours is weary work," and he yawned.

"I believe I should have been a clever fellow," mused the doctor, "if I had not been so confoundedly lazy. There's something very interesting in these cases. In yours, for instance, my fine old fellow, it sets one thinking whether I could have treated you differently, and whether I could do anything to prevent the recurrence of these fits."

He smoked on in silence, and then shook his head.

"No," he said, half aloud; "if there is a fire burning, and that is kept burning, all that we can do is to keep on smothering it for a time. It is sure to keep on eating its way out. He has a fire in his brain which he insists upon keeping burning, so until he quenches it himself, all I can do is to stop the flames by smothering it over by my medical sods. You must cure yourself, Norman Gartram ; I cannot cure you. No, and you cannot cure yourself, for you will go on struggling to make more money that you have no use for, till you die. Poor devil !"

He said the last two words aloud, in a voice full of pitying contempt. Then, after another sip of his coffee, he looked round for a book, drew the lamp close to his right shoulder, and picked up one or two volumes, but only to throw them down again ; and he was reaching over for another when his eye fell upon the cash belt with its bulging contents.

"Humph," he ejaculated, as he turned it over and over, and noted that it had been in service a long time. "Stuffed very full. Notes, I suppose. Old boy hates banking. Wonder how much there is in ? Very dishonourable," he muttered ; "extremely so, but he has placed himself in my hands."

He drew out a pocket-book.

"Wants a new elastic band, my dear Gartram. Out of order. I must prescribe a new

band. Let me see; what have we here?
Notes—fivers—tens—two fifties. Droll thing
that these flimsy looking scraps of paper should
represent so much money. More here too—
tens, all of them."

He drew forth from the pockets of the book
dirty doubled-up packets of Bank of England
notes, and carelessly examined them, refolding
them, and returning them to their places.

" What a capital fee I might pay myself,"
he said, with an unpleasant little laugh ; " and
I don't suppose, old fellow, that you would
miss it. Certainly, my dear Gartram, you
would be none the worse. Extremely one-
sided sometimes," he said, " to have had the
education of a gentleman and run short. Yes,
very."

He returned the last notes to the pocket,
and raised a little flap in the inner part.

" Humph ! what's this ? An old love letter.
No: man's handwriting :—' Instructions to my
executors.' "

He gave vent to a low whistle, glanced at
the sleeping man, then at the door, and back
at his patient before laying down the pocket-

book, and turning the soiled little envelope over and over.

"Not fastened down," he muttered. "I wonder what— Oh, no : one can't do that."

He hastily picked up the pocket-book, and thrust the note back into its receptacle, but snatched it out again, opened it quickly, and read half aloud certain of the sentences which caught his attention—"Granite closet behind book cases—vault under centre of study—big granite chest."

"Good heavens!" he said, after a pause, during which he read through the memorandum again ; then refolding it and returning it to the envelope, he hastily placed the writing in its receptacle, and in turn this was put in the pocket-book. Lastly, the book was returned to the pouch in the belt, which latter was thrust hastily into one of the drawers of the writing-table, the key turned and taken out.

"Give it to Mademoiselle Claude," he said, with a half laugh. "What an awkward thing if I had been tempted to behave as some would have done under the circumstances."

He took out a delicate lawn handkerchief,

unfolded it, and wiped the perspiration from his forehead, and then proceeded to do the same to his hands, which were cold and damp.

"That coffee is strong," he said, "or it is my fancy; perhaps the place is too warm."

He walked up and down the room two or three times, gazing anxiously at the bookshelves, and then at the table, where the floor was covered with a thick Turkey carpet; but he turned away and re-filled his cup with coffee and brandy, found that his cigar was out, and threw the stump away before helping himself to a fresh one, and smoking heavily for some time, evidently thinking deeply.

Then, apparently unable to resist the temptation, he rose and walked to the door, opened it and listened, found that all was silent, closed it again, and after glancing at his patient, who was sleeping heavily, he hastily drew out the key, opened the drawer, and, after a momentary hesitation, took out the belt.

In another minute, the yellow looking memorandum was in his hands, being studied carefully before it was restored to its resting-place, and again locked up.

"I did not know I had so much curiosity in my nature," he said, with a half laugh. "Well, the study of mankind is man, doesn't some one say, and I'm none the worse for a little extra knowledge of a friend's affairs. I might be called upon to give advice some day."

Oddly enough, the knowledge again affected the doctor so that he wiped his brow and hands carefully, and then sat gazing thoughtfully before him as he sipped and smoked and seemed to settle down into a calm, restful state, which at times approached drowsiness.

Upon these occasions he rose and softly paced the room, stopping to listen to his patient's breathing, and twice over feeling his pulse.

"Could not be going on better," he muttered.

Finally, during one of his turns up and down, he heard a step outside the door, followed by a light tap, and Claude entered.

The doctor started, and looked at her wildly

"Why have you come down?" he said.

"Come down? How is he? I overslept myself, and it is half-past two."

"Is it so late as that?"

"Doctor Asher!" cried Claude excitedly, as she caught him by the arm, "you are keeping something back."

Her words seemed to smite him, and he tried vainly to speak. It was as if he had suddenly been startled by some terrible shock, and he stared at Claude with his jaw slightly fallen.

"Why don't you speak?"

"Keeping something back," he said hoarsely. "No!"

"No? Why do you say that? You seem so confused and changed. Tell me, for heaven's sake; my father—"

"Better—better," he said, recovering himself, and speaking loudly, but in a husky voice. "I—I have been a little drowsy, I suppose, with the long watching. Not correct, but natural."

She looked at him wonderingly, he seemed so strange, and unable to contain herself, she turned to where her father lay, with her heart throbbing wildly, and something seemed to whisper to her the words, "He is dead."

CHAPTER VII.

SARAH WOODHAM'S VOW.

IT was after many hours of stupor, and when Doctor Asher, the physician of Danmouth, had gone back to the Fort, from a hurried visit to his injured patient, that Isaac Woodham unclosed his eyes, and lay gazing at the pale, agony-drawn face of his wife, upon which the light of the solitary candle fell.

"What's the matter?" he said hoarsely.

"Ike, husband," whispered the suffering woman.

"Oh, yes; I remember now," he said, with a piteous groan. "I always knew it would come."

"Ike, dear, can I do anything?" said his wife tenderly.

"Yes."

"Tell me what, dear?"

"I'll tell you soon," groaned the man. "I

knew it would come; I always felt it. Ah, my girl, my girl, I've preached to them often, and talked about the end of a good Christian man, but it's very, very hard to die."

"Die! oh, Isaac, don't say that."

"Yes; and to die through him—through that tyrant, and all to make him rich."

"No, no; you'll get better, dear, as Roberts did, and Jackson, who were worse than you."

"Hah!" he cried, making a gesticulation, as if to cast aside his wife's vain words; and then, with a sudden access of force that was startling, he caught at her hand.

"Sally, my lass," he whispered harshly, "Gartram has murdered me."

"Isaac, my poor husband, don't say that."

"It was all his doing. He always thwarted me, and interfered when I had to blast."

"Pray, pray be still, dear. You are so bad and weak. The doctor said you were to be kept quiet, and not to talk."

"Doctor knew it was all over. I am a dying man."

"No, no, my darling."

"Yes, I'll say it, and more too while I have

time. But for Gartram, I should be well and strong now. Oh, how I hate him! Curse him for a dog!"

"Isaac!—darling husband."

"Yes; I always hated him, the oppressor and tyrant. He made me mad about blasting that bit of rock, and I felt I must do it—my way; but he bullied me till my hands were all of a tremble, and I was thinking about what he said till I wasn't myself, and the stuff went off too soon. But it was his doing. He murdered me; and if it hadn't been for him, I should have been right."

"Oh, my darling!"

"Hush, don't cry, my lass. It's all over now, but I can't die peaceful like yet."

"Let me put your poor hands together, Ike, and I'll pray for you."

"Yes, my lass, but not yet. I'm dying, Sally—fast."

"No, no, Ike. There, let me give you a drop of the stuff the doctor left. It'll do you good."

"Nothing'll do me good but you."

"Ike, dear, be still and I'll run and fetch

the doctor; he's at the Fort.   Gartram has had a bad fit."

"Curse him!"

"No, no, dear, don't curse.   You make me shiver."

There was a terrible silence in the gloomy cottage room, where the ghastly face of the injured man seemed to loom out of the darkness, and looked weird and strange.   The woman tried to quit his side, but he held her tightly as he lay gazing straight up at her, his breath coming in a laboured way, as if he had to force each inspiration, suffering agony the while; and if ever the stamp of death was set plainly upon human countenance, it was upon his.

"Sally," he gasped, and his voice was changing rapidly.   "Sally!"

"Yes, dear."

"Don't leave me.   Where are you?"

"Here, darling; holding your hands."

"Why did you put out the light?"

"Isaac, my own dear man!"

"Listen.   Do you hear me?"

"Yes, dear, yes."

"I'm dying fast, and I shall never rest without—without you do what I say."

"Yes, dear, I'll do anything you tell me—you know I will."

"That's right. Quick, before it's too late."

"Oh, if help would only come," moaned the woman.

"No help can come, my lass. Now, put your hand under me and lift my head on your shoulder. That's right. Ah!"

He uttered a groan of agony, and lay speechless as she raised him; and the wife turned cold with horror, as it seemed to her that he was dead, but his lips moved again.

"Now," he said, " I can talk without feeling strangled. Gartram has made an end of me, and it's a dying man speaking to you. It's almost a voice from the dead telling you what to do."

"Yes, dear, tell me. What shall I do?"

"You'll swear to do what I tell you?"

"Yes, Isaac, anything."

"You're in the presence of death, wife, with the good and evil all about us, and what you say is registered against you."

" Yes, dear," said the woman, shuddering.

" You swear, so help you God, to obey my last words ? "

" Yes, dear," cried the woman, with her eyes lighting up, and a look of exultation in every feature ; " I'll swear to obey you."

" Then you will measure out to Norman Gartram, and pay back to him all he has paid to me."

" Isaac ! "

" An eye for an eye, a tooth for a tooth, as it says in the Holy Book."

" Husband ! "

" You have sworn to do it, woman, and there is no drawing back. As he murdered me, so you shall cut short his cursed life."

" Isaac, I cannot."

" Woman, you have sworn to the dying ; you are the instrument, the chosen vessel to execute God's wrath upon this man. For he shall not live to do more wrong to the suffering people he has been grinding under his heel."

" No, no : I could not do this thing, Isaac, it is too terrible."

" She has sworn to do it. She has heard

the message, and his days will come to an end as mine have come, and he will go on no longer in his wickedness, piling up riches. Ha! ha! ha! Thou fool—this night shall thy—wife—are you there?"

"Isaac! Husband!"

"Ah, yes. Good wife, my last words. Words from the other world. You will not rest till you have fulfilled your sacred task. I shall not rest till then—you—the chosen vessel—His wrath against the oppressor—as I have been—cut off—so shall Gartram be—cut off—yours the chosen hand, wife—quick—your hand—upon my head—you swear—that you will do my bidding—the bidding of—"

He paused, and she saw his eyes gazing wildly in hers, and it seemed as if the words she whispered were dragged from her—a voice within her seeming to utter them, and the belief that she was but the instrument of a great punishment upon a sinful man appeared to strengthen within her breast.

"Quick," gasped the dying man; "your hand upon my head, wife—your lips close to me—let me hear you speak."

"Isaac! Husband!" she groaned; "must I do this dreadful thing?"

"It is a message from—"

There was a terrible silence in the narrow chamber, and the dying man's eyes were fixed upon hers as she laid her hand upon his brow and spoke firmly,—

"I swear."

"Hah!"

A low, rattling expiration of the breath, and as Sarah Woodham gazed in her husband's eyes, the wild, fiery look died slowly out, to become grave and tender. Then it seemed to her that the look was fixed and strange. She had been prepared, but not for so sudden a shock as this.

"Ike!" she cried, lowering him upon the pillow. "Ike! Why don't you speak? Do you hear me?" and her voice sounded peremptory and harsh; "do you hear me?"

She had seized him by the shoulders as she bent over him, and her voice grew more excited and strange.

"You are doing this to frighten me—to keep that oath—but I will do it. Ike, dear, do you hear me? Don't play with me. It hurts my poor heart—to see you—so fixed and strange —Ike! Husband! Speak!"

In her horror and agony she gripped his shoulders more tightly and shook him.

Then the horrible truth refused to be kept longer at bay, and, starting back from the couch where the fixed, grave eyes seemed to follow her, reminding her of her oath, she stood with her hands raised, staring wildly for a few moments before an exceeding bitter cry escaped her lips.

"No," she cried; "it can't be. My darling, don't leave me here alone in the weary world. Isaac, my own! My God! he's dead."

She reeled, caught at the table to save her-self, the ill-supported candle dropped from the stick, and she fell with a thud upon the floor, as the candle rolled from the table close to her face, flickered for a few moments to display its ghastly lineaments, and then died out.

But it was not quite dark.

A faint light stole in beside the drawn-down blind, the chill air of morning sighed round the house, and a low murmur came from the waves fretting among the broken granite far below; and it was as if the night, too, were dead, and the low sigh died away in a hushed silence.

Then *pink, pink, pink, pink* came the sharp cry of the blackbird from the tangle of bramble and whortleberry high up the cliff slope, and from the grassy level above, the clear loud song of the lark, as it rose high in the pale morning sky, telling that come sorrow come joy, the world still goes round, and that Nature will have her way, even though murder be on the wing.

CHAPTER VIII.

CLAUDE OPENS THE AWFUL DOOR.

SARAH WOODHAM sat in her little parlour, sallow of cheek, and with a hard, stern look in her eyes as she gazed straight before her at the drawn-down blind, and listened to the mournful wash of the waves which came with a slow, regular pulsation through the open door.

Hers had been no romantic life. Hard working servant for years at the Fort, till, in a dry, matter-of-fact way, Isaac Woodham, quarryman, and local preacher at the little chapel, and one of the most narrow-minded and bigoted of his sect, had cast his eyes upon her in the chapel and preached to her. He had selected his texts from various parts of the Bible, where it was related that certain men took unto themselves wives, and when he was at work he told himself that Sarah was comely to look upon, and that one of these days he would marry her.

And so it was that previously, on one of these days when he had to go on business to the Fort, he had told the woman in his hard, matter-of-fact way that he had prayed for guidance, and that he felt it was his duty and her duty that they two should wed.

Sarah, in her hard, matter-of-fact way, asked for time to consider the matter herself, and at the end of a year's cold, business-like term of probation, she gave Isaac Woodham her hand, left the Fort, and went to live at one of the quarry cottages, which became at once the most spotless in the stone-cutters' hamlet by the sea.

They neither of them ever displayed any great affection one for the other, but led a quiet, childless, orderly life, in which she—with no pleasant recollections of her sojourn at the Fort, but still with a deep, almost motherly kind of affection for the girl whom she had seen grow up to womanhood—listened to and sided with her husband in his harsh revilings of his tyrant.

It was Isaac Woodham's never-failing theme —his hatred of his master, whom he looked

upon with the bitter, narrow-minded envy of
his nature. Every sharp word was magnified,
every business order was looked upon as an
insulting piece of tyranny, and after obeying
in a morose, sulky way, he took his revenge
by pitying the owner of the quarry, and
praying that he might repent and become
a better man.

This went on for years, during which Norman Gartram did not repent after his servant's
ideas of repentance ; and had he known the
circumstances, he would have said he had nothing to repent of, which, as far as his men
were concerned, was perfectly just—his greatest sins being the insistence upon receiving a
fair return for the wages he paid, and a rather
stern way of giving his orders to all, Woodham being the most trusted for his sterling
honesty, albeit Gartram sneered at him as
being full of cant.

Then came the catastrophe, with Sarah, the
newly-made widow, in her bereavement, feeling
that in her hard way she had dearly loved the
cold, stern man who had been her husband
those last few years ; and then she shivered as

she thought of the oath he had exacted from her, and felt that it was an order from the unseen world.

Her husband had nursed indifference into hatred, till she was as bitter against Gartram as he was himself; and years passed as the sharer of his troubles had made her so much akin that, like her husband, she was full of the bitter letter of the old Scriptures, without the under-current of the spirit of forgiveness and love.

And so it was that she sat there low in spirit, thinking of the few short hours that would elapse before friends would come and bear away the cold, stern-faced form of him who had been her all, straight to the little chapel-yard, with its rough granite walls, beyond the quarry, where he would be laid to rest, well within hearing of the waves, which would lull him in his long sleep, and near to where all day long rang out the crack of the heavy stone hammers, the ring of the tamping irons, and from time to time the sharp report and the following roar of some charge when a mass of the titanic granite was laid low.

Only a few days could elapse, she thought, before, in obedience to the new orders of a cruel master, she would have to leave the carefully kept cottage which had been her pride—the only pride to which she gave harbour in her breast.

And it would be better so, she thought. The sooner Gartram bade her turn out homeless, almost penniless in the world, the easier would be her task. It would give her fresh cause for hatred, a new stimulus for destroying the man who had caused her husband's death.

It was hour by hour, with the dead lying so near, becoming easier to her to think of Gartram as her husband's murderer. Isaac had with his dying lips insisted upon it that this was so, and he could not lie. The seed he had planted then was rapidly growing into a tree, and, accepting the task, she brooded over the deed she was to do, telling herself that it was to give immortal rest to him who was gone before; and once the task was accomplished, she prayed that she might soon rejoin him in the realms of bliss, and look him again in the eyes and say—" It is done."

How was it to be?

She sat there, with a strange, lurid light in her dark eyes, thinking over the vengeance and of those of whom she had read; of how Jael slew Sisera with the hammer and nail— that deadly enemy of the chosen race. Then of Judith; and a strange exultation filled her breast, and in her weak, ignorant way she began to feel herself more and more as one selected to become the instrument of Heaven's punishment upon one accursed.

"The way will be opened unto me," she said to herself. "The way will be opened unto me, and the wicked shall perish. Yes, husband, you shall rest in peace."

She started erect in her chair, and turned a fierce look of anger towards the door, as at that moment there was a light step, a shadow fell across the clean white stone, a sweet-toned, tremulous voice uttered her name, and there was the rustling of a dress upon the floor, while the next moment two soft arms were about her neck, her cheeks were wet with another's tears. For Claude was kneeling by her, with her head resting on the hard, heavily-beating heart, and the girl's broken voice fell upon her ears.

"My poor, poor Sarah! I could not come to you before. What can I do to help you? What can I say?"

Claude could not see the wild, agonised face, as she rested upon the trembling woman's breast. There had been kindly, sympathetic, neighbourly words enough spoken to her before, but these—the words of the girl she had years before tended and loved, winning her gentle young love in return—went straight to her overcharged heart. The tears falling for her sorrow seemed to quench the burning glow of bitterness and hate, and the next moment vengeance, and the determination to execute her husband's command, were swept away: her arms were tightening round the slight, girlish form as if it were something to which she could cling for safety, and the tears that had seemed dried up, after searing her brain, poured forth as she bent down sobbing hysterically, and in broken accents calling her visitor, "My darling bairn."

Half-an-hour had passed, and the bitter

wailing and hysterical cries had ceased, while
the suffering woman's breast heaved slowly
now, like the surface of the sea quieting after
a storm ; but she still held Claude tightly to
her, and rocked herself gently to and fro, as
in bygone years she had held the girl when
some trouble had brought her, motherless,
and smarting from some bitter scolding, to
seek for consolation and help.

The words came at last to break the silence
of the solitary place.

"It was like you to come, my darling, and I
shall never, never forget it. It was like you."

"You know I would have come to you
before, but poor papa has been so ill, and I
dared not come away. But he is better now,
and sitting up."

The mention of Gartram seemed to harden
the woman once more, and with a catching
sigh she sat up rigidly in her chair. The
thoughts of him who lay waiting in the next
chamber brought with them the terrible
scenes through which she had passed, and the
scale of tenderness which Claude had borne
down now rose upward to kick the beam.

" It was a terrible shock to him," continued Claude. " You have been too full of your own trouble to know, but he was seized with a fit, and when I reached home I thought he was dead."

The woman drew her breath hard, but did not speak; only sat frowning, her brow a maze of wrinkles, her lips drawn to a thin pink line, and her teeth set fast, gazing once more straight before her at the drawn-down blind.

" Hah !" she ejaculated at last. " It has all come to an end."

Claude started, and looked up in the woman's face, the words were spoken in so strange and hard a tone.

" I don't like to talk to you about the future, and hope," Claude said at last; " it seems such a vain kind of way to comfort any one in affliction."

" Yes; life is all affliction," said the woman bitterly; and she frowned now at the kneeling girl.

" No, no; you must not look at things like that, Sarah. But it is hard to bear. How well I remember coming to see your home directly you were married."

"Don't talk about it, child," said the woman hoarsely.

"No, we'll talk about something else; or will it not be kinder if I sit with you only, and stay as long as I can?"

"No," said the woman harshly. "Rennals will take poor Isaac's place. How soon will it be?"

"How soon?"

"Yes; how soon shall I have to turn out of my poor old home?"

"Don't talk about it now, Sarah," said Claude gently. "It will be terribly painful for you, I know."

"Painful!" said the woman, with a bitter laugh, "to go out once more into the cruel world. But a way will open," she added to herself; "the time will come."

Her face grew more stony of aspect moment by moment, as she gazed through her nearly closed eyelids straight before her, heedless of the fact that Claude had risen from her knees, and was holding one of her hands.

"Don't talk of the world so bitterly, Sarah, dear," said Claude gently. "I must go now."

"Yes," said the woman, in a harsh voice.

"Mary is sitting with papa till I go back, or she would have come with me. She sent her kindest and most sympathetic wishes to you. She is coming to see you soon."

"Yes," said the woman again, in the same strange, harsh way.

"You know you have many friends and well - wishers who will be only too glad to help you."

"Yes ; Norman Gartram, whose first thought is to turn me out of the home we have shared so long."

"Don't be unjust, Sarah, dear. Papa speaks harshly sometimes, but he has the welfare of all his people at heart."

"And casts me out on to the high road."

"Nonsense, dear," said Claude gently. "Don't speak in that bitter way, when we are all trying so hard to soften your terrible loss. Papa's business must go on ; and Rennals, naturally, takes poor Woodham's place. I thought it all over this morning, and I felt that you would consent."

"To give up the house? Of course; it is not mine."

"And would be of no use to you now."

"No;—but a way will open to me yet," she added to herself.

"Sarah, dear old friend, you could not live alone. You will come back to your own old place with us?"

"What?"

The woman sprang to her feet as if she had received some shock, then reeled, and would have fallen, but for Claude's quick aid.

"I have been too sudden. I ought to have waited, but I thought it would set your mind at rest."

"Say that again," whispered the woman, with her eyes closed.

"There is nothing to say. Papa will agree with me that it would be best to have our dear old servant back again; and, as soon as you can, you will come."

"No, no; no, no; it is impossible," cried the woman, with a shudder. "I could not return."

"You think so now; but papa will consent,

and I shall insist, too. But there will be no need to insist. It will be like coming back home."

"No, I tell you," cried the woman excitedly; and it was as if a wild fit of delirium had suddenly attacked her. "No, no, Isaac, darling, I cannot, I dare not do this thing."

"My poor old nurse," said Claude affectionately; "we will not talk about it now. You must wait, and think how it will be for the best."

"Be for the best!" she cried, in a wild strange way. "You do not know—you do not know."

"Oh, yes; better than you do, I am sure. Come, I will leave you now. Don't look so wildly at me. There, good-bye, dear old nurse —my dear old nurse. Kiss me, as you used when I was quite a child, and try to reconcile yourself to coming to us. It is fate."

Claude kissed her tenderly, and then, not daring to say more, she hurried from the darkened room, to walk swiftly back, glad that the loneliness of the cliff road enabled her to let tears have their free course for a time.

Could she have seen the interior of the cottage, she would have stared in wonder and dread, for, sobbing wildly and tearing at her breast, with all the unbridled grief of one of her class, Sarah Woodham was walking hurriedly to and fro, like some imprisoned creature trying to escape from the bars which hemmed it in.

"His child,"—she cried,—"his poor, innocent child to draw me there. What did she say? It is fate. Yes, it is fate; and we are but the instruments to work His will."

She stopped, gazing wildly towards the inner chamber, pausing irresolutely for a few moments before rushing in and flinging herself upon her knees by the dead.

It was an hour after that she came tottering out, to stand by the chair she had occupied, and by which she found a handkerchief Claude had dropped; and, catching it up, she pressed it to her lips.

"His poor, innocent child to lead me there to execute judgment on the evil doer. And I have prayed so hard—so hard—in vain—in vain. Yes, she is right. We are but instruments; and it is my fate."

She stood with her hands pressed to her brow, as if to keep her throbbing brain from bursting its bonds. Then a strangely-weird, despairing look came across her darkening face, and she let herself sink, as if it were vain to combat more; and there was a terrible silence in the place, as she seemed to be looking forward into the future.

Once again she broke that silence as the turn of her thoughts was made manifest, but her voice sounded harsh and broken, as if the words would hardly come.

"His innocent child—the girl I loved as if she had been my own flesh and blood;" and her voice rose to a wail. Then, after a few moments' silence: "Yes, I must go. I swore to the dead, and the way is opened now. It is my fate."

CHAPTER IX.

THE BEGGAR.

CHRISTOPHER LISLE sat in his snug, bachelor room at Danmouth, tying a fly with a proper amount of dubbing, hackle, and tinsel, for the deluding of some unfortunate salmon. The breakfast things were still on the table, and there was a cloud over his head, and another cloud in his brain.

The room was bright and pleasant, overlooked the sea, and was just such a place as a bachelor in comfortable circumstances, with a love for outdoor sports, would have called a snuggery. For it was just so tidy as not to be very untidy, with fishing and shooting gear in all directions; pipes in a rack, tobacco jars and cigar boxes on shelves; natural history specimens in trays and cabinets, from pinned beetles up to minerals and fossils; and under a table, in a case, lay Chris Lisle's largest

112

salmon, carefully cast and painted to fairly resemble life.

The tying of that fly did not progress, and after a good many stoppages it was thrown down impatiently.

" Confound the hook," cried Chris. " That's four times I've pricked my finger. Everything seems to go wrong. Now, what had I better do ? He ought to be well enough to see me now, and so better get it over. I'd no business to go on as I did ; but who could help it, bless her, holding her in my arms like that, and loving her as I do ? Wrong. Oh, it was honest human nature ; and any other fellow would have done the same.

" I suppose I ought to have spoken to the old man first. Though who in the world could think of him at a time like that. But how black he looked ; and then there was that confounded good-looking yachtsman there."

This was a point in the business which required thinking out ; and to do this thoroughly Chris Lisle took up a black pipe, filled it, and after lighting it daintily with a good deal of toying with the flame, he threw himself back in his chair, and began to frown and smoke.

"No," he said aloud, after a long pause. "Nonsense; the old fellow might think something of it, but my darling little Claude—never. And she's not the girl to flirt and play with any one. No; I know her too well for that—far too well. I frightened her, I was so sudden. A woman is so different to a man, and that wasn't put on; it was sheer timidity—poor little darling! How I do long to apologise, and ask her to forgive me. I must have seemed terribly awkward and boorish in her eyes, for I pulled up quite sulkily after that facer I got from Mary Dillon. The nasty, spiteful little minx. It was too bad. Fortune-hunter! Why, I'd marry Claudie without a penny, and be glad of the chance. Hang the old man's money. What do two young people, who love each other dearly, want with money?"

The idea seemed to be absurd, and he sat smoking dreamily for some minutes.

"I'll serve the spiteful, sharp-tongued little thing out for this," he said at last. "No, I will not. Rubbish! She didn't mean it. But I'll go up and hear how the old man is. He ought to be able to see me this morning, and I'll speak out plainly this time, and get it over."

Chris Lisle was not the man to hesitate. He threw aside his pipe, rang for the breakfast things to be cleared away, glanced at the looking-glass to see if he appeared decent, and stuck a straw hat on his crisp, curly hair.

"Not half such a good-looking chap as the yachtsman," he said, with a half laugh. "Glad of it. Wouldn't be such a smooth-looking dandy for the world. Why, hang it!" he said with a laugh, as he strode along by the rocky beach in the full tide of his manly vigour, "I could eat a fellow like that. I never thought of it before," he continued to himself, as he walked on. "Fortune-hunter! I can't be called a poor man. Two hundred and fifty a year. Why, I never felt short of money in my life. Always seemed to be enough for everything I wanted. Bah! nobody but little midges up there could ever say such a thing as that."

A peculiar change seemed just then to be taking place in Chris Lisle. The moment before he was swinging easily along, giving a friendly nod here and there to fishermen and loungers, who saluted him with a smile and a "Morn', Mr Chris, sir," the next he had grown stiff and rigid, as he saw a dingy pulled in to the landing-place some distance ahead, and Glyddyr leap out, the distance fitting so that the young men had to pass each other, which they did with a short nod of recognition.

"Swell!" muttered Chris contemptuously, as he strode on.

"Bumpkin!" thought Glyddyr, as he went in the other direction, and he laughed softly to himself.

A short distance farther along the cliff road Chris came suddenly upon a figure in deep mourning, and he stopped short, with his whole manner changing once more.

"Ah, Mrs Woodham," he said, in a low voice full of commiseration, "I have not been up to the quarry, but I had not forgotten an old friend. Can I be of any service to you?"

The woman shook her head.

"Don't do that," he said kindly. "They will not keep you, but recollect, Sarah, that we are very old friends, and I shall be hurt if you want money and don't come to me."

"God bless you, Master Chris," said the woman hoarsely; "but don't keep me now."

She hurried away, and he stood looking after her for a few moments.

"Poor thing!" he said, as he went on. "What trouble to have to bear. Hang it all, I wouldn't change places with Gartram if I could."

He went on, thinking deeply about Glyddyr.

"The old man seems to have quite taken to that fellow, and did from the first time he came here with his yacht. Regular sporting chap. Wins heavily on the turf. Bound to say he loses, too. Three hundred thousand pounds, they say, he had when his father died. Well, good luck to him! I hadn't when mine passed away."

Chris began to whistle softly as he went on, stopping once to pick a flower from out of a niche where the water trickled down from a crack in the granite, and, farther on, taking out a tiny lens to inspect a fly. Then another botanical specimen took his attention, and was transferred to a pocket-book, and by that time he was up at the castellated gateway and bridge over the well-filled moat of the Fort.

He went up to the entrance, with its nail-studded oaken door, just as he had been hundreds of times before since boyhood, rang, and walked into the hall before the servant had time to answer the bell.

"Anybody at home?" he said carelessly.

"Yes, sir; master's in the study, and the ladies are in the drawing-room."

"Mr Gartram well enough to see me, I suppose?"

"Oh, yes, sir. Doctor Asher was here to breakfast, and master's going out."

"All right; I'll go in."

There was no announcing. Chris Lisle felt quite at home there, and he crossed the stone-paved hall, gave a sharp tap at the study door, and walked in.

"Morning, sir," he cried cheerily. "Very glad to hear you are so much better."

"Thankye," said Gartram sourly; "but I'm not so much better."

"Get out," said Chris.

"What?"

"I mean in the open air."

"Oh. Well, Mr Lisle, what do you want—money?"

"I? No, sir. Well, yes, I do."

"Then you had better go to a lawyer. I have done all I could with your father's estate as your trustee, and if you want to raise money don't come to me."

"Well," said Chris, laughing, "I don't want to raise money, and I do come to you."

"What for, sir?"

"Well, I'll tell you," said Chris, speaking on the spur of the moment, for an idea had occurred to him. "But suppose we drop the 'sir'-ing. It doesn't seem to fit after having known me all these years."

"Go on. I'm not well. Say what you want briefly. I'm going out."

"I won't keep you long, but it may be for your benefit. Look here, guardian, you know what I have a year?"

"Perfectly—two hundred and fifty, if you haven't been mortgaging."

"Well, I haven't been mortgaging. It is not one of my pastimes. But it has occurred to me that I lead a very idle life."

"Bless my soul!" cried Gartram sarcastically. "When did you discover that?"

"And," continued Chris, "it seems to me that, as you are growing older—"

Gartram's face twitched.

"Your health is not anything like what it should be."

Gartram ground his teeth, but Chris was so intent upon his new idea that he noticed nothing, and went on in a frank, blundering, earnest way.

"Worse still, you have just lost, by that terrible accident, poor Woodham, who was your right-hand man. It would not be a bad thing for you, and it would be a capital thing for me, if you would take me on to be a sort of foreman or superintendent at the quarries. Of course, I don't mean to go tamping and blasting, but to see that the men did their work properly, that the stones were taken to the wharf, and generally to see to things when you were not there or wanted a rest."

"At a salary?"

"Salary? Well, I hadn't thought of that. But yes: at a salary. A labourer's worthy of his hire. It would make you more independent, and me too. Of course, I am not clever in your business, but I've watched the men from a boy, and I know pretty well how things ought to be done; and of course you could trust me as you could yourself."

Gartram's face was a study. His illness had exacerbated his temper, and over and over again, as the young man went on in his frank, blundering, honest fashion, he seemed on the point of breaking out. But Chris realised nothing of this. He only grew more sanguine as his new idea seemed to be brighter and more feasible the more he developed it, feeling the while that he was untying an awkward knot, and that his proposals would benefit all.

There was not a gleam of selfishness in his mind, and if Gartram had said: "I like your proposal, and I'll give you fourteen shillings a week to begin with," he would have accepted the paltry sum, and felt pleased.

"You see," he continued, "it would be the very thing; you want a superintendent who would take all the petty worries off your mind."

"And by-and-by," said Gartram, suffocating with wrath, "you would like me to offer you a partnership?"

Chris's eyes flashed.

"Yes, Mr Gartram, I should like that dearly. I never felt till just now that I was a poor man; my wants have been so simple. Yes, by-and-by, you might offer me a partnership if you found me worthy, and you should, sir; I swear you should."

"And with it my daughter's hand?"

"I was coming to that, Mr Gartram," said Chris flushing, and with a proud, happy look in his eyes, as he sat gazing straight out of the window to sea. "I felt, naturally, a shrinking about speaking of that, but Claude and I were boy and girl together. I always liked her, and that liking has grown into a man's honest, true love. I should have come to you before to explain about what you saw in the glen, but, of course, I felt how out of place anything would be from me at a time when you were in trouble and ill, and so I waited till this morning."

"Yes," said Gartram hoarsely; "go on."

"I know I ought not to have spoken to Claude as I did without first speaking to you, but it slipped out without thought, and I ought to say I am sorry, sir; but, feeling as I do, I can only say that I am glad."

"One moment," said Gartram, speaking perfectly calmly, but with a voice that sounded as if it were iced; "let us perfectly understand one another—you propose that I should engage you as my foreman?"

"Yes, Mr Gartram," said Chris quietly. "I have had the education of a gentleman—well, I may say it—my father was a gentleman. I am a gentleman, but I am not proud. I quite agree with you that a man should lead a useful life. I wish to lead a useful life."

"Exactly," continued Gartram; "to be my foreman at a salary, with a view to future partnership and my daughter's hand?"

" Yes, Mr Gartram ; and I will make your interests my study.   What do you say ? "

" Say ? " cried Gartram, in a voice of thunder. " Damn your impudence ! "

" What ! "

" You miserable, insolent, conceited young hound !   You come here with such a proposition, after daring, on the strength of the freedom I gave you of my house—for your father's sake—to insult my daughter as you did up that glen."

" Miss Gartram has not said I insulted her ? " cried Chris.

" I say insulted her with your silly, impudent talk about your love.   Why, confound it, sir, what are you—a fool, an idiot, or a conceited, presumptuous, artful beggar ? "

" Mr Gartram !—No, I will not be angry," said Chris, subduing the indignant rage which was in him.   " You have been ill and are irritable.   I have badly chosen my time.   Don't speak to me like that, sir.   I have always looked up to you as a guardian ever since I was left alone in the world.   You don't mean those words, sir. Say you don't mean them, for Claude's sake."

"Silence, sir! For Claude's sake, indeed. Confound you! How dare you! You must be mad to raise your eyes to her. You contemptible, artful, fortune-hunting scoundrel!"

"Mr Gartram!" cried Chris, flushing with anger now. "How dare you speak to me like this?"

"Because I am in my own house, sir. Because a miserable, mad-brained jackanapes has dared to make an attack upon me and upon my child. Silence—"

"Silence, sir, yourself!" raged Chris.

"What? You insolent dog, I'll have you turned out of the house. I'll have you horse-whipped. Dare so much as to speak to my child again. Dare so much as to look at her. Dare to come upon my premises again, and damme, sir, I'll—I'll shoot you!"

"You don't mean it. You shall not mean it," cried Chris hotly.

"Out of my house, sir!"

"Mr Gartram," cried Chris, as the old man, half mad with rage and excitement consequent

upon the reaction from his fit, strode close up
to where his visitor stood.

"I say out of my house, sir, before I have
you horse-whipped as I would a dog."

As he spoke, he gave the young man a thrust,
half blow, across the chest, just as the door
opened, and the servant announced Mr Glyddyr,
stood with open mouth, staring for a moment
at the scene, and then, as the new visitor
entered, ran back, without stopping to close
the door, to announce to Claude and Mary
that master was going to have another fit.

"Hah!" cried Gartram, as his eyes lit upon
Glyddyr; "you, is it? Look here," he roared,
in a voice choked with passion, "this beggarly,
insolent upstart—this puppy that I have
helped to rear—has had the audacity to propose for my daughter's hand."

"What?" cried Glyddyr, taking his tone
from Gartram; and, turning upon Chris, he
darted a look mingled of incredulity, threatening and contempt.

"Yes; I am weak from illness, or I'd ask no
man's help. You are young and strong. Take
him by the collar, and bundle the insolent

scoundrel neck and crop out of the place.
That's right : quick !"

Glyddyr advanced straight to where Chris
stood, with a blank look of rage and despair
upon his countenance, crushed, drooping, half
broken-hearted, as he felt how ingenuous he
had been to speak as he had to the hard,
grasping man of the world before him ; but as
Glyddyr laid his hand upon his collar, he
uttered a low, hoarse sound, like the growl
of an angry beast.

"Now, sir, out you go," cried Glyddyr, with
a mocking, sneering look in his countenance,
full of triumph. "Out with you before you
are kicked out."

"Take away your hand," said Chris, in a
low, husky whisper.

"What ! No insolence. Out with you !"

"Take away your hand."

"Do you hear me ? Now then, out."

"Curse you, you will have it, then," cried
Chris, shaking himself free ; and then, as
Glyddyr recovered himself, and tried to seize
him again, Chris's left fist darted out from
his shoulder, there was a low, dull sound, and

Glyddyr staggered back for a couple of yards, to fall with a heavy crash, just as, with a shriek of horror, Claude, closely followed by Mary, rushed into the room.

"Chris Lisle, what have you done?" cried Claude, while Mary, whom fate had made the busy help of the family, hurried to Glyddyr's side, and helped him to rise to a sitting position. He did not attempt to get upon his feet.

"Lost my temper, I suppose," said Chris, who began to calm down as he saw the effect of his blow. "But it was his own doing. I warned him to keep his hands off."

"Leave my house, ruffian, before I send for the police."

"You'll be sorry for all this, Mr Gartram," said Chris. "Claude—"

"Silence!" shouted Gartram. "Recollect, my girl, that henceforth this man and we are strangers. Everything between us is at an end. Once more, sir, will you leave my house?"

"Yes, I'll go," replied Chris slowly, as his eyes rested on Claude's. "Don't think ill of me," he said to her huskily. "I have done nothing wrong."

Gartram came between them, and, feeling that time alone could heal the terrible breach, Chris made a gesticulation and walked slowly to the door, where he turned.

"Mr Gartram," he said, "you'll bitterly repent this. But don't think that I shall give up. I'll go now. One of these days, when you have thought all over, you will ask me to come back, and we shall be friends again. Claude—Mary, all this was not my seeking. Good-bye."

"Not his seeking!" cried Gartram, sinking into a chair and dabbing his face with his handkerchief. "He wants to kill me : that's what he's trying to do. How are you now, Glyddyr? Pray forgive me for bringing this upon you. The scoundrel must be mad."

"Getting better now, sir," said Glyddyr ; and, as his enemy had gone, beginning with a great show of suffering and effort to suppress it, as his eyes sought sympathy from Claude. He found none, so directed his eyes at Mary, who offered him her hand as he made slowly for the nearest easy-chair. "I suppose I was a bit stunned. Not hurt much, I think."

"I don't know how to apologise enough,"

cried Gartram ; "and you two girls, have you nothing to say ? An outrageous assault on my guest ! But he shall smart for it. I'll have him summoned."

" No, no, Mr Gartram, I'm getting all right fast," said Glyddyr, quickly seizing the opportunity to be magnanimous in Claude's eyes. " Mr Lisle was excited, and he struck me. A blow like that is nothing."

" Mr Christopher Lisle will find out that a blow such as you've received means a great deal more than he thinks, sir. Claude, ring the bell. Have the spirit stand and soda-water brought in. Are you sure you are not seriously hurt, Glyddyr ? "

" Quite, sir : a mere nothing. Great pity it happened. Why, ladies, it must have regularly startled you. Miss Gartram, I am very sorry. You look pale."

" Enough to startle any woman, Glyddyr. But there, it's all over for the present. You had better leave us now, girls."

" No, no," cried Glyddyr, " don't let me drive them away, sir."

" It is not driving them away, Mr Glyddyr,"

said Gartram shortly. "I wish them to go."

"I beg pardon, I am sure."

"Granted, sir; but I like to be master in my own house."

"Papa, dear, pray, pray be calm," whispered Claude, who had crept to his side.

"Calm! Of course. I am calm. There, there, there; don't talk to me, but go, and I said ring for the spirit stand."

"Yes, papa, I did. I'll go and send it in."

"Yes, quickly. You are sure you would not like the doctor fetched, Glyddyr?"

"Oh, certain, sir. There, let it pass now. A mere nothing."

"Oh, my poor darling Claude," whispered Mary, taking her cousin's hand as they went out, and kissing her pale face as the large dark eyes gazed pitifully down in hers.

"Do you understand what it all means, Mary?"

"Only too well, coz: poor Chris has been telling uncle he loved you, and that put our dear tyrant in a passion. Then Mr Glddyyr came, and poor Chris got in a passion too, and knocked him down."

"Yes," sighed Claude; "I'm afraid that must be it."

"Yes, my dear, it's all cut and dried. You are to be Mrs Glyddyr as soon as they have settled it all."

"Never," said Claude, frowning and looking like a softened edition of her father.

"And as that sets poor Chris at liberty," continued Mary, with one of her mischievous looks, "and you don't want him, there may be a bit of a chance for poor little me."

"Mary, dear!" said Claude, in a voice full of remonstrance.

"It's rather bad taste of you, for though Mr Glyddyr is very handsome, I think Chris is the better man. Mr Glyddyr seems to me quite a coward making all that fuss, so that we might sympathise with him. Better have had poor Chris."

"Mary, dear, how can you make fun of everything when I am in such terrible trouble?"

"It's because I can't help it, Claude, I suppose. But oh, I am sorry for you if uncle makes you marry handsome Mr Glyddyr."

"Mary!"

"I cannot help it, dear; I must say it. He's a coward. He was hurt, of course, but not so much as he pretended. Chris Lisle knocked him right down, and he wouldn't get up for fear he should get knocked down again. Didn't Chris look like a lion?"

"It is all very, very terrible, Mary, and I want your help and sympathy so badly."

"I can't help you, coz; I'm too bad. And all this was my fault."

"No; not all," said Claude sadly. "Papa has been thinking about Mr Glyddyr for a long time, and dropping hints to me about him."

"Yes; and you'll have to take him."

"No," said Claude, with quiet firmness; and her father's stern, determined look came into her eyes. "No, I will never be Mr Glyddyr's wife."

"But uncle will never forgive poor Mr Lisle."

"Don't say that, Mary. Never is a terrible word. Papa loves me, and he would like to see me happy."

"And shall you tell him you love Chris?"

"No," said Claude sternly.

"If you please, ma'am, Mrs Woodham is

here," said one of the servants; and Claude's face grew more troubled as she asked herself what her father would say to the step she had taken, in bidding the unhappy woman come and resume her old position in the house.

She had not long to wait.

As she rose to cross the room she caught sight of Glyddyr looking back at the windows on leaving the house, and heard the study bell ring furiously.

"Quick, Mary!" she cried, as she rushed through the door, being under the impression that her father had had another seizure.

The relief was so great as she entered the study and found him standing in the middle of the room, that she threw herself in his arms.

"I thought you were taken ill again," she gasped, as she clung to him, trembling.

He was evidently in a fury, but his child's words were like oil upon the tempestuous waves.

"You—you thought that?" he said, holding her to his breast and patting her cheek tenderly. "You thought that, eh? And they say in

Danmouth that everybody hates me. That there isn't a soul here who wouldn't like to dance upon my grave."

"Papa, dear, don't talk like that."

"Why not? the ungrateful wretches! I've made Danmouth a prosperous place. I spend thousands a year in wages, and the dogs all turn upon me and are ready to rend the hand that feeds them. If they are not satisfied with their wages, they wait till I have some important contract on the way, and then they strike. I haven't patience with them."

"Father!" cried Claude firmly, "Doctor Asher said you were not to excite yourself in any way, or you would be ill."

"And a good thing, too. Better be ill, and die, and get out of the way. Hated—cursed by every living soul."

Claude clung more tightly to him, laid her head upon his breast, and placed her hand across his lips as if to keep him from speaking.

A smile came across the grim face, but there was no smile in his words as he went on fiercely, after removing the hand and seeming about to kiss it, but keeping it in his hand without.

"Everything seems to go against me," he cried. "Mr Glyddyr—just going—I was seeing him to the door, when, like a black ghost, up starts that woman Sarah Woodham. What does she want?"

"I'll tell you, dear, if you will sit down and be calm."

"How the devil can I be calm," he raved, "when I am regularly persecuted by folk like this?"

But he let Claude press him back into an easy-chair, while, feeling that she was better away, Mary Dillon crept softly out of the room.

"Well, then," he said, as if his child's touch was talismanic, and he lay back and closed his eyes, "I'll be calm. But you don't know, Claude, you can't tell how I'm persecuted. I'm robbed right and left."

"Papa, my dear father, you are as rich as ever you can be, so what does it matter?"

"Who says I'm rich? Nonsense! Absurd! And then look at the worries I have. All the trouble and inquest over that man's death, and through his sheer crass obstinacy."

" Why bring that up again, father, dear ? "

" Don't say father. Call me papa. Whenever you begin fathering me, it means that you are going to preach at me and bully me, and have your own way."

" Then, papa, dear, why bring that up again ? "

" I didn't. It's brought up and thrust under my very nose. Why is that woman here ? "

" Papa—"

" Now, it's of no use, Claude ; that man regularly committed suicide out of opposition to me. He destroyed a stone worth at least a hundred pounds by using that tearing dynamite, which smashes everything to pieces ; and then, forsooth, he charges me in his dying moments with murdering him, and the wretched pack under him take up the cry and bark as he did. Could anything be more unreasonable ? "

" No, dear, of course not. But the poor fellow was mad with agony and despair. It was so horrible for him, a hale, strong man, to be cut down in a moment."

" He cut himself down. It would not have happened if he had done as I ordered."

"You must forgive all that now. He knew no better; and as for the workmen, you know how easily they are influenced one way or the other."

"Oh, yes, I know them. And now this woman's here begging."

"No, papa, dear."

"I say she is. I could see it in her servile, shivering way, as soon as she caught my eye; now, look here, Claude, I sha'n't give her a shilling."

Claude held his hand to her cheek in silence.

"I won't pay for the man's funeral. I'm obliged to pay the doctor, because I contracted for him to attend the ungrateful hounds; but I will not help her in the least, and I'll have no more of your wretched tricks. I'm always finding out that you are helping the people and letting them think it is my doing. Now, then, I've done, and I want to be at peace, so go and send that woman away, or I shall be ill."

Claude clung a little more closely to her father, nestling, as it were, in his breast.

"Well," he said testily, "why don't you go?".

"My father is the leading man in this neighbourhood," said Claude, in a soft, soothing tone, "and the people don't know the goodness of his heart as I do."

"Now, Claudie, I won't have it. You are beginning to preach at me, and give me a dose of morals. My heart has grown as hard as granite."

"No, it has not," said Claude, kissing his veined hand. "It is as soft and good as ever, only you try to make it hard, and you say things you do not mean."

"Ah, now!" he shouted, "you are going to talk about that Lisle, and I will not have his cursed name mentioned in the—"

"I was not going to talk about Christopher Lisle," said Claude, in the same gentle, murmuring voice, whose tones seemed to soothe and quiet him down; "I was going on to say that I want the people—the weak, ignorant, easily-led people—about here to love and venerate my dear father's name."

"And they will not, do what you will. The

more you do for them, the less self-helpful they
are, and the more they revile and curse.   Why,
if I was ruined to-morrow, after they've eaten
my bread for years, I believe they'd light a
bonfire and have a dance."

"No, no ; no, no," murmured Claude.   "You
have done too much good for them."

"I haven't.   You did it all, you hussy, and
pretended it was I," he said grimly, as he
played with her glossy hair.

"I did it with your money, dear, and I am
your child.   I acted as I felt you would act
if you thoroughly knew the circumstances, but
you had no time.   What is the use of having
so much money if no good is done ?"

"For ungrateful people."

"We are taught to do good for evil, dear."

"What !" for a race of thieves who are
always cursing and reviling us ?   There, I'm
busy and tired, Claudie.   I've listened to your
moral lesson very patiently, and now I want
to be at rest.   But I forbid you to help that
wretched woman.   She and her husband
always hated me.   Confound 'em, they were
always insulting me.   How dare they—actu-

ally publicly insult me—in that miserable little chapel."

" Insulted you ? What do you mean ? "

" Why, they prayed for my heart to be softened, hang 'em ! "

" Oh, father, dear ! "

" There you go again. Papa—papa—papa. Don't forget that we do belong to the aristocracy after all. Now, go and send that dreadful woman away."

" I cannot, dear."

" Cannot ? "

" No, papa. She has come to stay."

" Sarah Woodham ? To stay ? Here ? "

" Yes, dear. Poor thing : she is left penniless, almost, for Woodham did not save."

" No, of course not. They none of them do."

" He spent all he had to spare," continued Claude, in the same gentle, murmuring tone, as she pressed her father's hand to her cheek. " Everything he could scrape together he gave to the poorer chapel people."

" Yes, I know ; in his bigoted way to teach me what to do. And don't keep on rubbing your cheek against my hand. Any one who saw you would think you were a cat."

"So, papa dear, as we want a good, trustworthy woman in the house, and Sarah was with us so long, and knew our ways so well, I arranged for her to come back."

"Claude!"

"Yes, dear; and these years of her married life, and the sad end, will be to her like a mournful dream."

"I—"

Norman Gartram made an angry gesture, but Claude's arms stole round his neck, her lips pressed his as she half lay upon his breast, and with the tears gently falling and hanging like pearls in his grisly beard, she said in a low, sweet voice,—

"And some day, father dear, at the last, as she thinks of what an asylum this has been to her, she will go down to her grave blessing your name for all the good that you have done, and this will make me very happy, dear, and so it will you."

There was a long silence in the room, and Norman Gartram's face began to grow less

rugged. It was as if there was something
of the same look as that in his child's, when,
with a tender kiss upon his brow, she left his
arms and half playfully whispered,—

"Am I to go and send Sarah Woodham
away ? "

"No," he said hastily, as his old look returned ; " you are as bad as your poor, dear
mother, every bit. No," he cried, with an
angry flush. " I won't do that, though. Not
a farthing of my money shall go towards
paying for that man's funeral."

" Father, dear—"

" Papa."

" Then papa, dear," said Claude quietly,
" I have paid everything connected with
poor Woodham's funeral."

" You have ? "

" Yes ; you are very generous to me with
money, and I had plenty to do that."

" Yes ; and stinted yourself in clothes. You
don't dress half well enough. Well, there,
it's done now, and we can't alter it. I suppose these people will think it was my doing."

" Yes, dear."

" Of course. Well, as to this woman, keep her and nurse and pamper her, and pay her the largest wages you can ; and mark my words, my pet, she'll turn round and worry us for what we have done."

" I have no fear, dear. I know Sarah Woodham too well, and I can do anything I like with her."

" Yes, as you can with me, you hussy," he cried. " Duke—King—why, I'm like water with you, Claude. But," he cried, shaking a finger at her, "there are things, though, in which I mean to have my way."

Claude flushed up, and a hard look came into her eyes.

But no more was said then.

CHAPTER X.

DENISE.

" WHAT the deuce brought you here ? "

" Train my boy. Saw in the shipping news that *The Fair Star* was lying in Danmouth. Felt a bit seedy, and knew that you would give me a berth aboard, and here I am."

" So I see."

" Well, don't be so gloriously glad, dear boy. Don't go out of your mind and embrace me. I hate to be kissed by a man ; it's so horribly French."

" Don't be a fool."

" Certainly not ; but you seemed to be in such raptures to meet me that I was obliged to protest."

" Now, look here, Gellow, it's not of the slightest use for you to hunt me about the country. I have no money, and I can't pay."

" I never said a single word about money, dear boy."

"No ; but you look money, and think money, and smell of money.   Good heavens, man, why don't you dress like a gentleman, and not come down to the seaside like the window of a pawn-broker's shop ? "

"Dress like a gentleman, sir ?   Why, I am dressed like a gentleman.   These are real diamond studs, sir.   First water.   Rings, chain, watch, everything of the very best. Never catch me wearing sham.   Look at those cuff studs.   As fine emeralds as you'd see."

"Bah !   Why don't you wear a diamond collar, and a crown.   I believe you'd like to hang yourself in chains."

"My dear Glyddyr, how confoundedly nasty you can be to the best friend you have in the world."

"Best enemy ; you are always hunting me for money."

"Yes ; and going back poorer.   You are such a one to wheedle a fresh loan."

"Yes ; at a hundred per cent."

"Tchah !   Nonsense !   But, I say, nothing wrong about the lady, is there ? "

" Hold your tongue, and mind your own business."

" Well, that is my business, you reckless young dog. If you don't make a rich match, where shall I be ? "

" Here, what are you doing ? "

" Ringing the bell, dear boy."

" What for ? "

" Well, that's cool. I have come all this way from town, had no end of trouble to run you down at your hotel, and then you think I don't want any breakfast."

" Yes, sir."

" Mr Glyddyr wants breakfast in directly. Here, what have you got ? No, never mind what you've got. I'll have broiled chicken and a sole. A fresh chicken cut up, mind ; none of your week-old, cooked stales. Coffee and brandy. Mr Glyddyr's order, you know."

The waiter glanced at Glyddyr where he sat pretending to read the paper, and receiving a short nod, he left the room.

" Now, once more, why have you come down ? "

" First and foremost, I have picked up three

or four good tips for Newmarket.   Chances for
you to make a pile."

" You are very generous," sneered Glyddyr.
" Your tips have not turned out so very rosy
so far."

" Well, of course it's speculation.   Have a
cigar ? "

Glyddyr made an impatient gesture.

" Then I will.   Give me an appetite for the
dejooney."

The speaker lit a strong cigar that had an
East London aroma, and went on chatting as
he lolled back in his chair, and played with
his enormously thick watch-chain.

" A smoke always gives me an appetite ;
spoils some people's.   Well, you won't take
the tips ?

" No ; I've no money for betting."

" Happy to oblige you, dear boy.   Eh ?
No !   All right.   Glad you are so independent.
It's going on bloomingly, then ? "

" What do you mean ? "

" The miller's lovely daughter," sang the visitor, laughingly.   " I mean the stonemason's."

Glyddyr muttered an oath between his teeth.

"Hush! Don't swear, dear boy — the waiter."

For at that moment the man brought in a tray, busied himself for a time till all was ready, and left the room.

"That's your sort," said Glyddyr's visitor, settling himself at the table. "Won't join me, I suppose? Won't have an echo?"

"What do you mean?"

"Second breakfast. Eh? No? All right. Hah! Very appetising after a long journey— confoundedly long journey. You do put up in such out of the way spots. Quite hard to find."

"Then stop away."

"No, thanks. Now look here, Glyddyr, dear boy, what's the use of your cutting up rusty when we are obliged to row so much in the same boat?"

"Curse you! I'd like to throw you overboard."

"Of course you would, my dear fellow, but you see you can't. Rather an awkward remark though, that, when I'm coming for a cruise with you in the yacht—my yacht."

Glyddyr crushed up the newspaper into a

ball, and cast it across to the corner of the room.

"What's the matter, old man? I say, what a delicious sole! Ever catch any on the yacht?"

The sound of Glyddyr's teeth grating could be plainly heard.

"Be no good to throw me overboard to feed the fishes, my dear boy. I'm thoroughly well insured, both as to money—and protection," he added meaningly. "Hope this fish was not fed in that peculiar way. *Tlat!* Capital coffee. Now then, talk. I can eat and listen. How is it going on with the girl?"

"Reuben Gellow, your insolence is insufferable."

"My dear Gellow, I must have a thou. to-morrow," said the visitor, mockingly. "Your words, dear boy, when you want money; the other when you don't want money. What a contrast! Well, I don't care. Capital butter this! It shows me that everything is progressing well with the pretty heiress, and that Parry Glyddyr, Esquire, will pay his debts like a gentleman. Come, old fellow, don't twist about in your chair like a skinned eel."

"Curse you, who skinned me?"

"Not I, dear boy. Half a dozen had had a turn at you, and that lovely epi—what-you-may-call-it of yours was hanging upon you in rags. I only stripped the rest off, so as to give you a chance to grow a new one, and I'm helping you to do it as fast as you can. Come, don't cut up rough. Be civil, and I'll keep you going in style so that you can marry her all right, and have two children and live happy ever after."

"Look here," said Glyddyr, getting up and pacing the room furiously, while his visitor calmly discussed his breakfast, "you have something under all this, so open it out."

"No, dear boy, only the natural desire to see how you are getting on. You owe me—"

"Curse what I owe you!"

"No, no, don't do that. Pay it."

"You know I cannot."

"Till you've made a good marriage; and you cannot live in style and make a good marriage without my help, my dear Glyddyr."

"You and your cursed fraternity hold plenty of security, so leave me in peace."

"I will, dear boy; but I want my trifle of money, and you are not getting on as fast as I could wish, so I've come to help you."

"Come to ruin me, you mean."

"Wrong. I have my cheque book in my pocket, and if you want a few hundreds to carry on the war, here they are."

"At the old rate," sneered Glyddyr.

"No, my dear fellow. I must have a little more. The risk is big."

"Yes. Might fail, and blow out my brains."

"Ex—actly! How I do like this country cream."

Glyddyr threw himself into his seat with a crash.

"That was all a metaphor," he said bitterly.

"What was, dear boy?"

"About the Devil and Dr Faustus."

"Of course it was. Why?"

"Faustus was some poor devil hard up, and the other was not a devil at all, but a con-founded money-lender. It was a bill Faustus accepted, not a contract."

"I daresay you are right, Glyddyr. Have a drop of brandy? Eh? No? Well, there's nothing like a *chasse* with a good breakfast, and this is really prime."

"Well, I'll grin and bear it till I'm free," said Glyddyr. "You want to know how I am getting on. You need not stay."

"But I want a change, and I can help you, perhaps."

"You'll queer the whole affair if you stay here. Once it is so much as suspected that I am not as well off as I was—"

"That you are an utter beggar—I mean a rum beggar."

"Do you want me to wring your neck?"

"The neck of the goose that lays the golden eggs? No. They don't kill geese that way."

"—The whole affair will be off."

"Old man's a rum one, isn't he?"

"How do you know?"

"How do I know?" said Gellow, with a quiet chuckle. "That's my business. I know everything about you, my dear boy. I have a great personal interest in your proceedings, and every move is reported to me."

"And, to make matters worse, you have yourself come down to play the spy."

"Not a bit of it, my dear Glyddyr; but you have cursed and bullied me at such a tremendous rate, that, as I have you on the hook, I can't help playing you a little."

"Oh!" snarled Glyddyr furiously.

"But, all the same, I am the best friend you have in the world."

"It's a lie!"

"Is it? Well, we shall see. I want you to marry King Gartram's daughter, and I'll let you have all you want to carry it out. And by the way, here are three letters for you."

He took the letters out of his pocket-book, and handed them.

"There you are: Parry Glyddyr, Esq., care of Reuben Gellow, Esq., 209 Cecil Street, Strand."

"Why, they've been opened!"

"Yes, all three—and read."

"You scoundrel!" roared Glyddyr. "Do you dare to sit there and tell me that you have had the effrontery to open my letters and read them?"

"I didn't tell you so."

"But you have read them?"

"Every line."

"Look here, sir," cried Glyddyr, rising fiercely, "I found it necessary to have my letters sent to an agent."

"Reuben Gellow."

"To be forwarded to me where I might be yachting."

"So as to throw your creditors off the scent."

"And you, acting as my agent, have read them."

"In your interest, dear boy."

"Curse you! I don't care what happens now. All is at an end between us, you miserable—"

"Go it, old fellow, if it does you good; but I didn't open the letters."

"Then who did?"

"Denise."

Glyddyr's jaw dropped.

"Now, then, you volcanic eruption of a man; who's your friend, eh? I went down to the office yesterday morning. 'Lady waiting in your room, sir,' says my clerk. 'Who is it?' says I. 'Wouldn't give her name,' says my clerk. 'Wants money then,' says I to myself; and goes up, and there was Madame Denise just finishing reading number three."

"Good heavens!" muttered Glyddyr, blankly.

"'I came, sare,' she says, with one of her pretty, mocking laughs, 'to ask you for ze address of my hosband, but you are absent. It ees no mattair. I find tree of my hosband's lettaires, and one say he sup-poz my hosband go to Danmout. Dat is all.'"

"Then she'll find me out, and come down here and spoil all."

"Divil a doubt of it, me boy, as Paddy says."

"But you—you left the letters lying about."

"Not I. They came by the morning's post. How the deuce could I tell that she would hunt me up, and then open her 'hosband's' letters."

"I am not her husband," cried Glyddyr furiously. "That confounded French marriage does not count."

"That's what you've got to make her believe, my dear boy."

"And if it did, I'd sooner smother myself than live with the wretched harpy."

"Yes; I should say she had a temper, Glyddyr. So under the circumstances, dear boy, I thought the best thing I could do was to come down fast as I could and put you on your guard."

" My dear Gellow."

" Come, that's better. Then we are brothers once again," cried Gellow, with mock melodramatic fervour.

" Curse the woman!"

" Better still; much better than cursing me."

" Don't fool, man. Can't you see that this will be perfect destruction?"

" Quite so, dear boy; and now that this inner man is refreshed with food, so kindly and courteously supplied by you, he is quite ready for action. What are you going to do?"

"I don't know. Think she will come down?"

" Think? No, I don't. Ah, Parry Glyddyr, what a pity it is you have been such a wicked young man!"

" Do you want to drive me mad with your foolery?"

" No; only to act. There, don't make a fuss about it. The first thing is to throw her off the scent. She knows you may be here."

" Yes."

" Well, she'll come down and inquire for you. She is not obliged to know about the people at the Fort; your yacht put in here for victualling or repairs."

" Well ?"

" When she comes, she finds you have sailed, and if we are lucky she will feel that she has missed you, and go back."

" If she would only die !" muttered Glyddyr, but his visitor caught his words.

" Not likely to. Sort of woman with stuff enough in her to last to a hundred. It strikes me, dear boy, that you are in a fix."

Glyddyr sat frowning.

" And now you see the value of a friend."

" Yes," said Glyddyr thoughtfully. " I must go."

" And you must take me too. If she sees me, she will smell a rat."

" Yes, confound you, and one of the worst sort. There, ring that bell."

" What for—brandy ? Plenty here."

" No, man, for the bill; I must be off at once."

CHAPTER XI.

As Burns said, matters go very awkwardly sometimes for those who plot and plan—as if some malicious genius took delight in thwarting the most carefully-laid designs, and tangling matters up, till the undoing seems hopeless.

Chris Lisle had had a bad time mentally. He was wroth against Gartram and Glyddyr, and far more wroth with himself for letting his anger get the better of him.

"It was as if I had made up my mind to fight against my own interests, for I could not have done that man a greater service than to strike him.

"That's it, sure enough," he said. "This good-looking yachting dandy is the man, and it was enough to make poor Claudie think me a violent ruffian, upon whom she must never look again. But I will not give her up. I'd

159

sooner die; and, bless her, she will never allow herself to be forced into marrying such a man as that, good-looking as he is. Well, we shall see."

To go up to the Fort and apologise seemed to him impossible, and he spent his time wandering about the shore, the pier, harbour and rocks, everywhere, so that he could keep an eye on Glyddyr's proceedings.

He told himself that he merely went down to breathe the fresh air, but the air never seemed to be worth breathing if he could not watch the different trimly-rigged yachts lying in the harbour, the smartest and best kept one of all being *The Fair Star.*

Glyddyr stayed at the hotel while his yacht was in the harbour, and Chris avoided that hotel on principle; but all the same he seemed to be attracted to it, and several times over the young men had met, to pass each other with a scowl, but they had not spoken since the day they had encountered up at the Fort.

There was a lurking hope, though, in Chris's breast, that sooner or later he would meet Claude, and come to an explanation.

"Just to ask her," he said, "to wait. I
know I'm poor ; at least, I suppose I am, but
I'll get over that, and force myself somehow
into a position that shall satisfy the old man.
He will not be so hard upon me when he sees
what I have done.   How unlucky in my choice
of time.   He was in a horrible fit of irritability
from his illness, and I spoke to him like a weak
boy.   I ought to have known better."

Just then he caught sight of a dress in the
distance, and his heart began to beat fast.

"It's Claude !" he exclaimed, and he increased his pace.

"No, it is not," he said, slackening directly.
"Stranger."

If he could have seen two hundred yards
farther, and round a corner, he would not have
checked his pace, but then his were ordinary
eyes, and he continued his course, looking half-
inquiringly at the figure which had attracted
his attention, and gradually grew more curious
as he became aware of the fact that the lady
was fashionably dressed, and very elegant in
her carriage.

The next minute he saw that she was young,

and almost directly that she was very handsome, while, to complete his surprise, she smiled, showing her white teeth, and stopped short.

"I demand your pardon, monsieur," she said, in a particularly rich, sweet voice, and pronouncing the words with a very foreign accent, "but I am so strange at zis place. I want ze small ship yacht *Ze Fair Star*. You will tell me?"

"Oh, certainly," said Chris quickly; "one, two, three, four," he continued pointing to where several graceful-looking yachts swung at their buoys. "That is it, the fourth from the left."

"Ah, but yes, I see. One—two—tree—four, and zat is *Ze Fair Star?*"

There was something droll and yet prettily piquant about her way of speaking, and in spite of himself Chris smiled, and the stranger laughed a little silvery laugh.

"I say someting founay, *n'est-ce pas?*" she said.

"I beg your pardon," cried Chris. "I don't think I made myself understood."

" Ah, perfectly. I am not Engleesh, but I understand. I count one, two, tree, four, and zat is *Ze Fair Star*, nombair four. Is it not so ? "

" Quite right," said Chris.

" But how shall I get to him ? "

" You must go down to the landing-place and hail her, or else hire a boatman to take you to her."

" Hail ! What is hail ? "

" Call—shout to the men on board."

" But, yes : I am vairay stupide. But where is ze boat to take me. I am so strange here at zis place."

" If you will allow me, I will show you."

" Ah, I tank you so much," and in the most matter-of-fact way, the stranger walked beside Chris towards the harbour, smiling and chatting pleasantly.

" I make you laugh vairay much," she said merrily ; and then, " aha ! ze *charmante* young lady is your friend. I will find my own way now."

She looked curiously at Chris, who had suddenly turned scarlet and then ghastly pale, for at the lane leading to the harbour they had come upon Claude and Mary, both looking wonderingly at him and his companion, and passing on without heeding his hurried salute.

"No, no," said Chris, recovering himself quickly ; and there was a flash of anger in his eyes as he continued rather viciously, "I will see you to the harbour, and speak to one of the boatmen for you."

"I thank you so vairay much," she said ; "but I understand you wish to go back to ze two ladies."

"You are mistaken," he said coldly ; "this way, please. It is very awkward for a stranger, and especially for a foreign lady."

She smiled, looking at him curiously, and, aware that they were the object of every gaze, Chris walked on by her trying to be perfectly cool and collected ; but, as he replied to his companion's remarks, feeling more awkward than he had ever felt in his life, and growing moment by moment more absent as in spite of his efforts he wondered what Claude would think, and whether he could overtake her afterwards and explain.

"I am French, and we speak quite plain, what we do tink," she said laughingly ; " here you have been vairay good to me, but you want to go to ze ladies we encounter ; is it not so ?—Ah ! "

The laughing look changed to one full of vindictive anger, as she muttered that quick, sharp cry, and increased the pace almost to a run.

Chris stared after his companion, seeming to ask himself whether she was a mad woman, but almost at the same moment he caught sight of Glyddyr and a showily - dressed stranger, just at the end of the little half-moon shaped granite pier which sheltered the few fishing luggers, brigs and schooners, and formed the only harbour for many miles along the coast.

They were sixty or eighty yards away, and as he saw Chris's late companion running towards them, Glyddyr stepped down from the harbour wall, and, with less activity, his companion followed, that being a spot where some rough granite steps led down to the water, and where boats coming and going from the yachts were moored.

Chris stood still for a moment or two, and then, carried away by an intense desire to see the end of the little adventure, he walked slowly down towards the pier, gradually coming in sight of Glyddyr and his companion, as the little gig into which they had descended was pulled steadily out towards the yacht.

There were plenty of loungers close up by the houses beneath the cliff, and sailors seated about the decks of the vessels, but the pier was occupied only by the handsomely-dressed woman, who increased her pace to a run, and only paused at the end, where she stood gesticulating angrily, beating one well-gloved hand in the other as she called upon the occupants of the boat to stop.

The stranger looked back at her and raised his hat, but Glyddyr sat immovable in the stern, looking straight out to sea, while the sailors bent to their oars, and made the water foam.

Chris stopped short some thirty yards from the end.

"It is no business of mine," he thought. " Is this one of Mr Glyddyr's friends ?"

Then he felt a thrill of excitement run
through him as he heard the woman shriek
out, shaking her fist threateningly,—

"*Lâche! Lâche!*" And then in quick,
passionate, broken English, "You will not
stop? I come to you."

Chris heard a shout behind him, and stood
for a few moments as if petrified, for, with
a shrill cry, the woman sprang right off the
pier, and he saw the water splash out, glittering in the morning sun.

Then once more a thrill of excitement ran
through him, as, thinking to himself that
there would be ten feet of water off there at
that time of the tide, and that it was running
like a mill-race by the end of the pier, he
dashed along as fast as he could go, casting
off his loose flannel jacket and straw hat,
bearing a little to his left, and plunging from
the pier end into the clear tide.

As he rose from his dive, he shook his
head, and saw a hand beating the water a
dozen yards away; then this disappeared, and
a patch of bright silk, inflated like a bladder,
rose to the surface, and then two hands ap-

peared, and, for a moment or two, the white face of the woman.

All the time Chris was swimming vigorously in pursuit.

The tide carried him along well, and as he made the water foam with his vigorous strokes, he took in the fact that Glyddyr was standing up in the gig, and that his companion was gesticulating and calling upon the men to row back. The pier, too, was resounding with the trampling of feet, and men were shouting orders as they came running down.

There was plenty of help at hand, but Chris knew that there was time for any one to drown before a boat could be manned, cast off and rowed to the rescue. If help was to come to the half-mad woman, it must be first from him, and then from Glyddyr's gig, which seemed to be stationary, as far as the swimmer could see.

But he had no time for further thought; his every effort was directed to reaching the drowning woman, and it seemed an age before he mastered the distance between them, and

then it was just as she disappeared. But,
raising himself up, he made a quick turn, and
dived down and caught hold of the stiff
silken dress, to rise the next moment, and
then engage in an awkward struggle, for first
one and then another clinging hand paralysed
his efforts. He tried to shake himself clear
and get hold of the drowning woman free
from her hands, but it was in vain. She
clung to him with the energy of despair, and,
in spite of his efforts to keep his head up,
he was borne down by the swift tide; the
strangling water bubbled in his nostrils, and
there was a low thundering in his ears.

A few vigorous kicks took him to the surface again, and, in his helplessness, he looked
wildly round for help, to see that Glyddyr's
gig was still some distance away; but the
men were backing water, and the stranger was
leaning over the stern, holding the boat-hook
towards them.

Then the tide closed over his head again,
and a chilling sense of horror came upon him;
but once more the dim shades of the water
gave place to the light of day, and he man-

aged to get partially free, and again to make desperate strokes to keep himself on the surface.

But he felt that his strength was going, and that, unless help came quickly, there was to be the end.

A shout away on the left sent a momentary accession of strength through him, and he fought desperately, but in vain, for again his arm was pinioned, and the water rolled over his head just as he felt a sharp jerk, and, half-insensible, he was drawn up to the stern of a boat.

What happened during the next few minutes was a blank. Then Chris found himself being lifted up the rough granite steps on to the pier, amidst the cheering of a crowd; and in a hoarse voice he gasped,—

"The lady; is she safe?"

"All right, Mr Lisle, sir," cried one of the men. "She's all square."

Then a strange voice close to his ear said hastily,—

"Yes; all right. You go."

He did not realise what it meant for a few

moments, but as he was struggling to his feet, to stand, weak and dripping, in the midst of a pool of water, the same voice said,—

" That's right, my lad. Carry her up to my hotel."

" No, no, my lads," cried Chris confusedly to the too willing crowd of fishermen about him ; " I'm all right. I can walk. Who has my jacket and hat ? "

" Here, what's all this ? " said another voice, as some one came pushing through the crowd.

" Only a bit of an accident, sir," said the same strange voice. " Lady—friend of mine —too late for the boat—slipped off the end of the pier."

" And Mr Chris Lisle saved her, sir."

" Humph ! Whose boat is that — Mr Glyddyr's ? "

" Yes, friend of mine, sir," said the same strange voice. " There, don't lose time, my lads. Quick, carry her to my hotel."

" Can I be of any assistance ? " said another voice.

" No, thank you. I can manage."

" Nonsense, sir ; the lady's insensible. Asher, you'd better go with them to the hotel."

Chris heard no more, but stood looking confusedly after the crowd following the woman he had saved, and as he began to recover himself a little more, he realised that the strange voice was that of the over-dressed man who had been in Glyddyr's boat, and that Gartram and then Doctor Asher had come down the pier, and had gone back to the cliff road, while he, though he hardly realised the fact that it was he—so strangely confused he felt—was seated on one of the low stone mooring posts, with a rough fisherman's arm about his waist, and the houses on the cliff and the boats in the harbour going round and round.

" Come, howd up, brave lad," said a rough voice.

" Here, drink a tot o' this, Master Lisle, sir," said another, and a pannikin was held to his lips.

" Seems to me he wants the doctor, too," said another.

" Nay, he'll be all right directly. That's it, my lad. That's the real stuff to put life into you. Now you can walk home, can't you ? A good rub and a run, and you'll be all right. I've been drownded seven times, I have, and a drop of that allus brought me to."

" That's very strong," gasped Chris, as he coughed a little.

" Ay, 'tis," said the rough seaman, who had administered the dose. " It's stuff as the 'cise forgot to put the dooty on."

" I can stand now," said Chris, as the sense of confusion and giddiness passed off; and when he rose to his feet, the first thing he caught sight of was Glyddyr's gig, by where the yacht was moored.

" Who saved me ? "

" That gent in Captain Glyddyr's boat, my son. Got a howd on you with the boat-hook, and, my word, he's given you a fine scrape. Torn the flannel, too."

" Thank you, thank you. I can manage now."

" No, you can't, sir. You're as giddy as a split dog-fish. You keep à hold on my arm.

That's your sort. I'll walk home with you. Very plucky on you, sir. That gent's wife, I suppose ? "

" Eh ? Yes. I don't know."

" Didn't want to be left behind, I s'pose. Well, all I can say is, he'd ha' been a widower if it warn't for you."

By this time they were at the shore end of the pier, but Chris still felt weak and giddy, and leaned heavily upon the rough seaman's arm, walking slowly homeward, with quite a procession of blue-jerseyed fishers and sailors behind.

Then, as from out of a mist in front he caught a gleam of a woman's dress, and the blood flushed to his pale face as he saw that Claude was coming toward him, but stopped short, and it was Mary Dillon's hand that was laid upon his arm, and her voice which was asking how he was.

CHAPTER XII.

THE GIFT OF A WHITE CARD.

A HASTY note had been despatched to the Fort by Glyddyr, announcing that a friend had come down from town, and that to entertain him he was going to take him for a short cruise in his yacht. Then there were the customary hopes that Gartram was better, and with kindest regards to Miss Gartram, Glyddyr remained his very sincerely.

"I don't like going off like this," grumbled Glyddyr ; "it looks as if I were being scared away."

"Well, that is curious," said Gellow, with mock seriousness.

"And it's like retreating from the field and leaving it to Lisle."

"Who the deuce is Lisle ? "

"Eh ? A man I know. Had a bit of a quarrel with him," said Glyddyr hastily.

"Quarrel ? What about ? "

" Oh, nothing, nothing."

Gellow talked in a light, bantering strain, but behind the mask of lightness he assumed, a keen observer would have noticed that he was all on the strain to notice everything, and he noted that there was something under Glyddyr's careless way of turning the subject aside.

" Rival, of course," thought Gellow.

They were walking down toward the pier, and as they neared the sea Glyddyr's pace grew slower, and his indecision more marked.

" I can't afford to trifle with this affair," he said. " I don't think I'll go."

" Well, don't go. Stop and order a nice piquant delicate little dinner in case Madame Denise comes, something of the *Trois Frères Provençaux* style, and I'll stop and dine with you, play gooseberry, and keep you from quarrelling."

" Come along," said Glyddyr sharply ; " we'll go, but I believe she will not come. No, I won't go. Suppose she does come down, and I'm not here, and she begins to make inquiries ? "

" Bosh ! If she comes and finds you are not here, the first inquiry she makes will be for when you went away, the second, for where you went."

" Possibly."

" Then let drop to some one that you are going to Redport, or Rainsbury, and she'll make at once for there."

" Confound you !" cried Glyddyr sharply. " Nature must have meant you for a fox."

" You said a rat just now, dear boy. I never studied Darwin. Have it your own way. That our boat ?"

" That's my boat," said Glyddyr sharply, as they reached the end of the pier.

" In with you, then," cried Gellow ; and then, in a voice loud enough to be heard on the nearest brig in the harbour, " Think the wind will hold good for Redport ?"

Glyddyr growled, and followed his companion into the boat, which was pushed off directly.

" I don't believe she'll come down," he whispered to Gellow, as the two sailors bent to their oars, and the boat began to surge through the clear water.

" Not likely," said Gellow. " Look ! "

Glyddyr gave a hasty glance back, and saw that which made him sit fast staring straight before him, and say, in a quick low voice,—

" Give way, my lads ; I want to get on board."

Then followed the excited appearance of the lady at the end of the pier, the cries to them to stop, and the plunge into the water.

" Well, she is a tartar," whispered Gellow.

" Don't look back, man."

" Oh, all right. Water isn't deep, I suppose ?"

" Look, sir," cried one of the sailors. " Shall we row back ?"

" No ; go on."

" Water's ten foot deep, sir, and the tide's running like mad," cried the man excitedly.

" Some one will help the lady out," said Glyddyr hastily. " Plenty of hands there."

" Hooray ! " cried one of the men, as Chris leaped off the pier.

" Tell them to back water," whispered Gellow excitedly. " It's murder, man."

Glyddyr made no reply, but seemed as if stricken with paralysis, as he looked back with a strangely confused set of thoughts struggling together in his brain, foremost among which, and mastering all the others, was one that seemed to suggest that fate was saving him from endless difficulties, for if the woman whom he could see being swept away by the swift current sank, to rise no more, before his boat reached her, his future would be assured.

He made a feeble effort, though, to save the drowning pair, giving orders in a half-hearted way, trembling violently the while, and unable to crush the hope that the attempt might be unsuccessful.

The men backed water rapidly, and Gellow raised the boat-hook, holding it well out over the stern in time to make the sharp snatch, which took effect in Chris's back, and holding on till more help came and they reached the pier.

"It's all over," whispered Glyddyr bitterly, as willing hands dragged Chris and his insensible companion up the steps.

"Not it," was whispered back. "Will you leave yourself in my hands?"

"I am in them already."

"Don't fool," said Gellow quickly. "You have got to marry that girl for your own sake."

"And for yours."

"Call it so if you like; but will you trust me to get you out of this scrape?"

"Yes, curse you: do what you like."

"Bless you, then, my dear boy; off you go."

"What do you mean?"

"Be off to the yacht, set sail, and don't come back to Danmouth till I tell you it's safe."

"Do you mean this?"

"Of course. But keep me posted as to your whereabouts."

"Here?"

"No; in town."

"But what are you going to do?"

"Fight for your interests, and mine. That woman's my wife, come down after me, and I'm going to take her home. See?"

"Not quite."

"Then stop blind. Be off, quick."

This hurried colloquy took place in the boat

by the rough granite stairs, the attention of those about being taken up by the two half-drowned people on the pier, the excited talk making the words inaudible save to those concerned.

"Now, then," whispered Gellow, "you'll leave it to me?"

"Yes," said Glyddyr, hesitating.

"*Carte blanche?*"

"You'll do nothing—"

He did not finish the sentence.

"*Carte blanche?*" said Gellow again.

"Well, yes."

"Right; and every lie I tell goes down to your account, dear boy. Bye-bye. Off you go," he said aloud, as he sprang on the stones. "I'm very sorry, Glyddyr; I apologise. If I had known she would follow me, I wouldn't have come."

"Give way," said Glyddyr, thrusting the boat from the steps; and he sank down in the stern, heedless of the dripping seat, and thinking deeply as the pier seemed to slip away from him, and with it the woman who had for years been, as he styled it, his curse.

He only glanced back once, and saw that Chris Lisle was being helped up into a sitting position, but the little crowd closed round him, and he saw no more, but sat staring hard at his yacht, and seeing only the face of the woman just drawn from the sea.

Then he seemed to see Chris recovering, and taking advantage of his absence to ruin all his hopes with Claude.

"If these two, Claude and Denise, should meet and talk," he thought.

"If Gartram should learn everything. If Denise should not recover. Hah!"

Glyddyr uttered a low expiration of the breath, as he recalled how closely Gellow's interests were mixed up with his own.

"And I have given him *carte blanche*," he thought; "and he will say or do anything to throw them off the scent—or *do* anything," he repeated, after a pause. "No, he dare do no harm; he is too fond of his own neck."

He had come to this point when he reached the side of his long, graceful-looking yacht, and as soon as he was aboard he gave his orders; the mooring ropes were cast off, and the sails hoisted.   Then, fetching a glass from the cabin, Glyddyr carefully scanned the pier and shore, but could see nothing but little knots of people standing about discussing the adventure, while the largest knots hung about the door of the hotel.

Almost at the same moment, Gellow was using the telescope in the hotel-hall.

" Right," he said to himself, as he closed it, upon seeing that the sails of the yacht were being hoisted.   " Good boy; but you'll have to pay for it.   Well, doctor, how is she ? "

Doctor Asher had just come down from one of the bed-chambers.

" Recovering fast," said that gentleman, following Gellow into a private room, " but very much excited.   She will require rest and great care for some days."

Gellow tapped him on the breast, and gave him a meaning look.

" No, she won't, doctor," he said, in a low voice.   " I must get her home at once.   Most painful for us both to stop.   People chattering and staring, and that sort of thing.   Most grateful to you for your attention," he continued, taking out his pocket-book, opening it quickly, and drawing therefrom two crisp new five-pound notes. Let me see, you doctors prefer guineas," he said, thrusting his hand into his pocket.

" No, no, really," protested Asher, as his eyes sparkled at the sight of the notes.

" Ah, well, I shall not press you, doctor ; but I'm down and you are down after this painful affair, so what do you say to prescribing for us both pints of good cham. and a seltzer, eh ? Not bad, eh ?"

" Excellent, I'm sure," said Asher, smiling ; " but really I cannot think of—er—one note is ample."

" Bosh, sir !" cried Gellow, crumpling up both, and pressing them into the doctor's hand. " Professional knowledge must be paid for. Here, waiter ; wine-list. That's right. Bottle of—of—of—of— Oh, here we are. Dry Monopole and two seltzers—no, one will do. Must practise economy ; eh, doctor ?"

The waiter hurried out, and Gellow continued confidentially,—

" Bless her ! Charming woman, but bit of

a tyrant, sir. Love her like mad don't half express it ; but there are times when a man does like a run alone. Just off with a friend for a bit of a cruise when the check-string was pulled tight. You understand ? "

" Oh, yes ; I begin to understand."

" Ah, here's the stimulus, and I'm sure we require it."

Pop !

" Thanks, waiter. Needn't wait. Now, doctor : bless her—the dear thing's health. Hah, not bad—for the country. I may take her back to-day, eh ? "

" Well, er—if great care were taken, and you broke the journey if the lady seemed worse—I —er—think perhaps you might risk it," said Asher, setting down his empty glass. " Of course you would take every precaution."

" Who would take more, doctor ? Put out, of course ; but the weaker sex, eh ? Yes, the weaker sex."

He refilled the doctor's glass and his own.

" An accident. Pray, don't think it was anything else ; and, I say : you will contradict any one who says otherwise ? "

" Of course, of course."

" There are disagreeable people who might say that the poor dear sprang off the pier in a fit of temper at being left behind, but we know better, eh, doctor ? "

" Oh, of course," said Asher, playing with and enjoying his glass of champagne.

" It's a wonderful thing, temper. Take a cigar ? "

" Thanks, no. I never smoke in the day-time."

" Sorry for you, doctor. Professional reasons, I suppose ? "

Asher bowed.

" I was going to say," continued Gellow, carefully selecting one out of the four cigars he carried, for no earthly reason, since he would smoke all the others in their turn. " I was going to say that it is a wonderful thing how Nature always gives the most beautiful women the worst tempers."

" Compensation ? " hazarded Asher.

" Eh ? Yes ; I suppose so. Going, doctor ? "

" Yes ; other patients to see."

" Then my eternal gratitude, sir, for what

you have done, and with all due respect to you and your skill, I hope I may never have to place a certain lady in your care again. Shake hands, my dear sir. Doctor Asher, I think you are called? That name will be engraven on the lady's heart."

"You will take the greatest care?" said Asher.

"Of course."

"And break the journey, if needful?"

"And break the journey if I think it needful. You need be under no apprehension, my dear doctor. Good morning, and good-bye.

"Yes; bless her! I'll take the greatest care, Asher, by gad!" said Gellow to himself, as he saw the doctor pass the window, when he filled his own glass, took a hasty sip, and then drew out his pocket-book.

"Shall I make a lump charge on this journey," he said, "or put down the separate items? Better be exact," he muttered, and he carefully wrote down,—

"Doctor's fees, twenty guineas; lunch for doctor, one guinea."

" Always as well to be correct," he muttered, as he replaced his pencil in the book, and drew round the elastic band with a snap. How am I to know about how she is going on ? By jingo !"

He started, so sudden was the apparition of the woman, who flung open the door, and closed it loudly, being evidently in a fierce fit of excitement and rage.

" Where is my hosband ? " she cried, speaking in a low voice, and through her teeth.

Gellow beckoned her to the window, and pointed out to where *The Fair Star* was careening over, with a pleasant breeze sending her rapidly through the water.

" He is dere," she said, watching the yacht through her half-closed eyes.

" Yes, he's off. Gave me the slip while I was helping you. By jingo, ma'am, you had a narrow escape."

" And you came down here to reveal him 'I was coming," she said, turning upon him suddenly, with her eyes widely open and flashing.

" Come, I like that," he replied, with cool

effrontery. "How the dickens should I know that you were coming down here?"

She did not reply, but stood gazing at him searchingly.

"But I wish to goodness you hadn't come."

"And why, monsieur, do you wish that I shall not come?"

"Because you spoil sport. Do you know that Glyddyr owes me thousands?"

"Of francs? He is vairay extravagant."

"Francs, be hanged! Pounds. I came down here to try and get some, and just as I'd got him safe, and he was taking me aboard his yacht to give me some money, you came and had that accident."

"Yais, I come and had that ac—ceedon," said the woman through her teeth. "Where to is he gone, monsieur?"

"Glyddyr? Ah! that's what I should like to know. Going to sail back to London, I expect. Gravesend, perhaps. How are you now?"

"He will come back here?" said the woman, paying no heed to the question.

Gellow burst into a roar of laughter.

"What for you laugh?" said the woman

angrily. "Am so I redeeculose in dese robe which do not fit me ?"

"Eh ? Oh, no. 'Pon honour I never noticed your dress. With a face like yours one does not see anything else."

"Aha, I see," said the woman, raising her eyebrows. "You flatter me, monsieur. I am extreme oblige. You tell me my face is handsome ?"

"Yes ; and no mistake."

"You tell me somting else I do not know at all."

"Eh ? Oh, very well. I will when I think of it."

"You tell me now. What for you laugh ?"

"Eh, why did I laugh ?"

The woman screwed up her eyelids, and nodded her head a great deal.

"I remember now. It was at your thinking that Glyddyr would come back here."

"He has sail away in his leettler sheep— in his yacht. Why will he not come back to-night, to-morrow, the next day ?"

"Shall I tell you ?"

"Yes ; you shall tell me."

" Because he will say to himself : ' No, I will not go back to Danmouth, because Madame Denise is so fond of me she will be waiting.' Do you understand ? "

"Oh, yais. I understand quite well. You sneer me, but you are his friend. You are his friend."

"Ha, ha, ha," laughed Gellow ; "you wouldn't have said that if you had heard him when I talked about money."

" Well ? "

The abrupt question was so sudden, that Gellow looked at the speaker wonderingly.

" Well what ? " he said.

" Why do you look at me ? Why do you ask me question ? You go your way, I go mine. I want my hosband. I will have my hosband. Why is he here ? "

"He isn't here," said Gellow, in reply to the fierce question.

" No, I know dat ; and you know what I mean. Why comes he here ? "

" Well," said Gellow, " I should think it was so as to get out of my way, and—now, don't be offended if I tell you the truth."

"Bah! I know you. You cannot offend me."

"Well, I'm sorry I am so insignificant in madame's beautiful eyes."

"What?"

"I say I am sorry I am so insignificant, but I'll tell you all the same. I should say that Mr Parry Glyddyr came down to this delectable, out-of-the-way spot so as to be where Mademoiselle Denise—"

"Madame Denise Glyd—dyr, sare."

"Ah, that's what Glyddyr says you are not."

"What?"

"I beg your pardon; I only tell you what he says."

"We shall see," cried the woman, stamping her foot, "what you did not finish yourself?"

"And I don't mean to," said Gellow, *sotto voce.*

"Well?"

"I have no more to say, only that I believe he came here so as to avoid you, and he is off somewhere now to be away from you."

"Yes, it is true," said the woman bitterly.

" If you had not come down, I daresay he
would have run back here."

" What for ? "

" How should I know ? Play billiards, read
the odds."

" He has a wife here, then."

" Do you mean Madame Denise ? " said
Gellow innocently.

She gave him a scornful look.

" Are you fool, or make fon of me ? " she
cried fiercely. " Bah, I am too much angry,
Is there a lady here ? "

" No, I should think not, but we could easily
find out. If he has, it is too bad, owing me
so much as he does. No, I don't think so ;
stop—yes I do. By Jingo, it's too bad. That's
why he did not want to take me out in his
yacht."

" What do you mean ? " said the woman
searchingly.

" If there is one, madame—if he is married,
she is aboard his yacht, and yonder they go—
no, they don't ; they're out of sight."

There was so much reality in Gellow's
delivery of this speech, that his *vis-à-vis* was

completely hoodwinked. She tried to pass it off with a laugh, but the compression of her lips, the contraction about her eyes, all showed the jealous rage she was in ; and it was only by giving one foot a fierce stamp on the carpet, and by walking quickly to the window, that she could keep herself from shrieking aloud.

" Well, madame," said Gellow, " you are getting all right again "

" Oh, yais ; I am getting all right."

" And you can do without my services ? "

" Oh, yais."

" Then I'll say good-bye. Glad I was near to help you out. Glad to see you again if you like to give me a call in town."

" Where are you going ? "

" Going ? Back to London as fast as I can."

" And what for, sir ? "

" To read up all the yachting news, and see where *The Fair Star* puts in, and then run down and give Master Glyddyr a bit of my mind."

" Stop—an hour—two hours."

" What for ? "

" Till I get back my dress all a dry. I go back wiz you."

" Oh, certainly, if you wish it; but I wouldn't; you had better stop here and rest for a few days—a week. I'll write and tell you all I find out."

" I go back wiz you," said the woman decidedly. And she kept her word, for in two hours they caught a train.

The next day came a telegram from Underley, giving that as Glyddyr's temporary address.

Gellow wrote back advising that the yacht should in future sail under another name, with her owner incog., and he added that the coast at Danmouth was now clear.

CHAPTER XIII.

HEARTS ARE NOT DEFORMED.

"Now Claude, darling, what do you think of me?" said Mary, one morning; "am I beautiful as a flower in spring?"

"No," said Claude gravely; "only what you are, my dear little cousin; why?"

Mary's face was flushed, and her eyes were sparkling as much from mischief as pleasure as she caught her cousin's hand, led her softly to the open window of her bedroom, and pointed down.

Claude looked at her wonderingly, but she was too well used to her companion's whims to oppose her, and she looked down.

"Can you see the goose?" whispered Mary.

"I can see Mr Trevithick walking with papa; I thought they were in the study;" and, she hardly knew why, she gazed down with some little interest at the tall, stoutish man of

196

thirty, with closely-cut dark hair and smoothly shaved face, which gave him rather the aspect of a giant boy as he walked beside Gartram, talking to him slowly and earnestly, evidently upon some business matter.

"Well, that's who I mean," said Mary, laughing almost hysterically, "for he must be mad."

"Now, Mary dear, what fit is this?" cried Claude, pressing her hands and drawing her away, as, a very child for the moment, she was about to get upon a chair and peep down from behind the curtain. "I know how angry papa would be if he caught sight of you looking down."

"Well, the man should not be such a goose —gander, I mean. I thought he was such a clever, staid, serious lawyer that uncle trusted him deeply."

"Of course," said Claude warmly ; "and he's quite worthy of it. I like Mr Trevithick very, very much."

"Oh !" exclaimed Mary, in a mock tragic tone, as she flung her cousin's hands away, "you'll make me hate you.'

"Mary, you ought to have been an actress."

"You mean I ought to have been a man and an actor, Claudie. Oh, how I could have played Richard the Third."

"Hush!"

"Oh, they can't hear. They're talking of bills and bonds and lading. I heard them. But Claude, oh! and you professing to love Chris Lisle."

"I never professed anything of the kind," cried Claude indignantly.

"Your eyes did; and all the time uncle is engaging you to Mr Glyddyr."

"Mary! For shame!"

"And in spite of this double-dealing, you must want Mr Trevithick, too?"

"Do you wish to make me angry?"

"Do you wish to make me jealous?"

"Jealous? Absurd!"

"Of course," cried Mary sharply. "What should a poor little miserable like I am know of love or jealousy or heartaches, and the rest of it?"

"My dear coz," whispered Claude, placing an arm round her, "I shall never understand you."

" There isn't much of me, Claude. It oughtn't to take you long."

" But it does," said Claude playfully. " I never know when you are serious and when you are teasing. I have not the most remote idea of what you mean now."

" Then I'll tell you. He's in love."

" Who is ? "

" Mr Trevithick."

" Mary ! "

" There you go. No : not with you. Of course, it would be quite natural if the great big fellow, coming here every now and then, had fallen in love with his client's beautiful daughter. But the foolish goose has fallen in love with some one else."

" Mary, dear, how do you know ? With whom ? "

" Ah ! Of course, you would never guess —with poor Mary Dillon."

" Oh, Mary, darling ! But has he really told you so ? "

" I should like to see him dare."

" Yes," said Claude quietly ; " I suppose that is what most girls would like."

"Don't, Claude dearest; pray don't. My sedate and lovely cousin trying to make jokes. Oh! this is too delicious. But it won't do, Claudie; it is not in your way at all. I am a natural, born female jester—a sort of Josephine Miller; but—you! oh, it is too ridiculous."

"Now, tell me seriously, what does this mean?" said Claude, taking the girl's hands.

"What I told you, darling. Big, clever, serious Mr Trevithick, the learned lawyer, is in love—with me."

"Mary, you must be serious now. But how do you know?"

"How do I know?" cried Mary, with a curl of the lip. "How does a woman know when a man loves her?"

"By his telling her so, I suppose; and you say Mr Trevithick has not told you."

"Didn't you know Chris Lisle loved you before he dared to tell—I mean, to give you instructions in the art of catching salmon?"

Claude was silent.

"No, of course you did not, dear," said Mary mockingly. "As if it was not only too easy to tell."

"But, Mary dear, this is too serious to trifle about. You have not given him any encouragement?"

"Only been as sharp and disagreeable to him as I could."

"But how has he shown it?"

"Lots of ways. Held my poor little tiny hand in his great big ugly paw, where it looked like a splash of cream in a trencher, and forgot to let it go when he was talking to me; looked down at me as if he were hungry, and I was something good to eat—like an ogre who wanted to pick my bones; sighed like the wind in Logan cave, and when I dragged my hand away, all crushed and crumpled up, and without a bit of feeling left in it, he begged my pardon, and looked ashamed of himself."

"And what did you say?"

"I? I said, 'Oh!'"

"That all?"

"No; I said, 'You've quite spoiled that hand, Mr Trevithick,' and then the monster looked frightened of me."

"I am very sorry—no, very glad, Mary,"

said Claude thoughtfully, and looking her surprise.

" Which, dear ? "

There was a tap at the door, and Sarah Woodham entered.

" Master wished me to tell you that Mr Trevithick will not stay dinner, Miss Claude, and said would you come down."

" Directly, Sarah," said Claude, rising. " You will not come, Mary ? " she whispered.

" Indeed, but I shall."

" Mary, dear," protested her cousin.

" Why, if I stop away the monster will think all sort of things ; that I care for him, that he has impressed me favourably, that I have gone to my room to dream. No, my dear coz, there are some things which must be nipped in the bud, and this is one of them. It is his whim—his maggot. Oh, Claude, he is six feet two. What a huge maggot to nip."

They were already part of the way down, to find Gartram and his great legal man of business standing in the hall.

"Better alter your mind, Trevithick, and have a chop with us. Try and persuade him, Claude."

"We shall be extremely glad, Mr Trevithick," said Claude; but her words did not sound warm, and her father looked at her as if surprised.

"I am greatly obliged, but I must get back to town," said their visitor; and he spoke in a heavy, bashful way, and looked at Mary as if expecting her to speak, but she did not even glance at him.

"Well," said Gartram, "if you must, you must."

The big lawyer looked at Claude again in a disappointed way, and his eyes seemed to say, "Coax me a little more."

But Claude felt pained as she glanced from one to the other, for there was something too incongruous in the idea of those two becoming engaged, for her to wish to aid the matter in the slightest way, and she held out her hand for the parting.

"I suppose it will be three months before we see you again, Mr Trevithick," she said.

" Yes, Miss Gartram, three months ; unless," he added hastily, " Mr Gartram should summon me before."

"No fear, Trevithick; four days a year devoted to legal matters are quite enough for me."

" We none of us know, Mr Gartram," said the big man solemnly. "Good-day, Miss Gartram ; good-day, Miss Dillon," and he shook hands with both slowly, as if unwillingly, before he strode away.

"I don't think Trevithick is well," said Gartram.

CHAPTER XIV.

A TELEGRAM.

THE same old repetition in Chris Lisle's brain : " How am I to grow rich enough to satisfy the King ? "

Always that question, to which no answer came.

Then would come, till he was half maddened by the thought, the idea that Glyddyr had returned after a few days' absence and had the free run of the Fort, and would be always at Claude's side.

" Constant dropping will wear a stone," he would say to himself; " and she is not a stone. I am sure she loved me, and I might have been happy if I had not been so cursedly poor —no, I mean, if she had not been so cruelly rich. For I am not poor, and I never felt poor till now. But I can't afford to keep a yacht, and go here and there to races, and win money. He must win a great deal at these races.

"Why cannot I?" he said half aloud, after a long, thoughtful pause. She would think no better of me, but the old man would.

"Surely I ought to be as clever as Mr Parry Glyddyr. I ought to be a match for him. Well, I am in brute strength. Pish! what nonsense one does dream of at a time like this. I can think of no means of making money, only of plenty of ways of losing it. Nature meant me for an idler and dreamer by the beautiful river, so I may as well go out and idle and dream, instead of moping here, grumbling at my fate.

"It's a fine morning, as the writer said; let's go out and kill something."

He stepped out into the passage, lifted down his salmon rod from where it hung upon a couple of hooks, took his straw hat, in whose crown, carefully twisted up, were sundry salmon flies, thrust his gaff hook through the loop of a strap, and started off along the front of the houses, in full view of the row of fishermen, who were propping their backs up against the cliff rail.

Plenty of "Mornin's" greeted him, with smiles and friendly nods, and then, as he walked on, the idlers discussed the probabilities of his getting a good salmon or two that morning.

Away in the sheltered bay lay Glyddyr's yacht, looking the perfection of trimness ; and as it caught his eye, Chris turned angrily away, wondering whether the owner was up at the Fort, or on board.

Just as he reached the river which cut the little town in two, he saw the boy who did duty as telegraph messenger go along up the path which led away to the Fort, and with the habit born of living in a little gossiping village, Chris found himself thinking about the telegraph message.

"Big order for stone," he said to himself as he studied the water. "How money does pour in for those who don't want it."

But soon after he saw the boy returning, a red telegraph envelope in his hand, and that he was trotting on quickly, as if in search of an owner.

"Not at home," he muttered; and then he became interested in the boy's proceedings in in spite of himself, as he saw the young messenger go down to the end of the rough pier and stop, as if speaking to some one below, before coming quickly back, and finally passing him, going up the path by the river side, as if to reach the old stone bridge some hundred yards up the glen.

"Gartram must be over at his new quarry," said Chris to himself, and as the boy disappeared, he thought no more of the incident till about fifty yards farther, as he had turned up by the bank of the river, he caught sight of him again.

He forgot him the next moment, for his interest was taken up by the rushing water, and he watched numberless little falls and eddies, as he went on, till, as he neared the bridge, he caught sight of a well-known figure seated upon the parapet smoking, and in the act of taking the telegram from the boy.

He tore it open and read the message, crumpled it up, and with an angry gesture threw it behind him into the stream; and as he pitched the boy a small coin, Chris saw the little crumpled-up ball of paper go sailing down towards the sea.

For a moment the young man felt disposed to avoid meeting Glyddyr, as, to reach the fishing ground he had marked down, he would have to go over the bridge, and then along the rugged path on the other side.

" And if he sees me going back, he'll think I'm afraid of him," muttered Chris.

At the thought, he swung his long lithe rod over his shoulder, and strode on, his heavy fishing boots sounding loudly on the rugged stones.

As Chris reached the bridge, Glyddyr was busy with his match-box lighting a fresh cigar, and did not look up till the other was only a few yards away, when he raised his head, saw who was coming, and changed colour. hen the two young men gazed fiercely into each other's eyes, the look telling plainly enough that what had passed and was going on made them enemies for life.

Chris tramped on, keeping his head up, and naturally, as he did not turn towards his rear,

he was soon out of eyeshot, when the sharp
report of a yacht's gun rang out from behind
him, the effect being that he turned sharply
round to look at the smoke rising half a mile
away.

It was a perfectly natural action, but Chris
forgot that he was carrying a long, elastic
salmon rod, and the effect was curious, for the
rod swung through the air with a loud *whish*,
and gave Glyddyr a smart blow on the cheek.

"I beg your pardon," cried Chris involuntarily, as Glyddyr sprang from the parapet
into the roadway, with a menacing look in his
eyes.

"You cad!" he roared. "You did that on
purpose."

"No, I did not," said Chris, quite as hotly.
"If I had meant to do it, I should have used
the butt of the rod, and knocked you over
into the river."

Glyddyr's lips seemed to contract till his
white teeth were bare; and, dashing down
cigar and match, he advanced towards Chris
with his fists clenched, till he was within a
couple of feet of his rival.

Chris's face grew set and stony looking, but he did not move. One hand held the rod, and the other was in his pocket, so that he offered an easy mark for a blow such as he felt would pay him back for the one which had sent Glyddyr over in the study at the Fort.

But he knew that the blow would not come, and a curiously mocking smile slowly dawned upon his lip as he saw that Glyddyr was trembling with impotent rage, and dared not strike.

" Well ? " said Chris. " Have you any more to say ? "

" You shall pay bitterly for these insults," whispered Glyddyr ; for he could not speak aloud.

" When you like, Mr Glyddyr," said Chris coolly ; " but you dare not ask me for payment. I told you that blow was an accident —so it was."

" You lie ! "

Chris flushed.

" Do I ? " he said hoarsely. " A minute ago I was sorry that I had struck you inadvertantly, and I apologised as a gentleman should."

"A gentleman!" said Glyddyr mockingly.

"Yes, sir, a gentleman; but you called me a cad and a liar, so now I tell you I'm glad I did strike you, and that it wouldn't take much to make me undo the rod and use the second joint to give you a good thrashing. Good morning."

There was a peculiar sound in the still sunny glen heard above the dull rush and murmur of the river. It was the grating together of Glyddyr's teeth, as Chris turned round once more, and unintentionally brushed the top of his rod against his rival again.

Glyddyr made a sharp movement, as if to snatch hold of and break the rod, but his hand did not go near it; and he stood there watching the fisherman as he turned down to the waterside, and went on up the glen, soon disappearing among the birches and luxuriant growth of heath and fern which crowned the stones.

"Curse him!" muttered Glyddyr, picking up the fallen cigar and lighting it, without smoking for a few minutes. "I'll pay him out yet. Well," he said, with a bitter laugh,

" I'm going the right way. Poor devil ; how mad he is. He shall see me come away from the church some day with little Claude on my arm, and I'd give a hundred pounds—if I'd got it—to let him see me take her in my arms, and cover her pretty face with kisses."

There was a peculiarly malignant screw in his face as he stood looking up the glen, and then he laughed again.

"Poor devil," he cried. "I can afford to grin at him."

He turned to go, and at that moment a puff of wind came down the glen, rustling a piece of paper in the road, and drawing his attention to the fact that it was the envelope of the telegram.

Then he stooped and picked it up, and shaped it out till it was somewhat in the form of a boat, as he dropped it over the stone parapet, and stood watching as it swept round and round in an eddy, and then went sailing down the stream.

"That's the way to serve you, Master Gellow," he muttered ; "and I wish you were with it sailing away out yonder. No, no, my fine fellow, once bit twice shy; once bit—a hundred times bit, but I've grown too cunning for you at last. Now, I suppose some other scoundrel is in that with you. Back it. Not this time, my fine fellow; not this time."

He smoked away furiously as he watched the scrap of paper float down, now fast, now slowly. At one time it was gliding down some water slide, to plunge into a little foaming pool at the bottom, where it sailed round and round before it reached the edge and was whirled away again. Now it caught against a stone, and was nearly swamped; now it recovered itself, and was swept towards the side, but only to be snatched away, and go gliding down once more in company with iridescent bubbles and patches of foam.

"Hah!" ejaculated Glyddyr, "if I only had now all that I have fooled away by taking their confounded tips, and backing the favourites they have sent me. No, Master Gellow, I'm deep in enough now, and I'm not the gudgeon to take that bait. Money, money. There'll be a fresh demand directly, and the old bills to renew. How easy it is to borrow, and how hard to pay it back. If I only had a few hundreds now, how pleasant times would be, and how easy it would be to get what I want."

Oddly enough, just at the same time, Chris Lisle was busily whipping away at the stream in foaming patch and in dark gliding pool, thinking deeply.

"Such a despicable coward!" he muttered. "Why, if a man had served me so, I should have half killed him. What a fate for her if it were possible, and here is he accepted by that sordid old wretch of a fellow, just because he has money. Now, if I had a few thousands! Ha!"

He whipped away, fishing with most patient energy till he reached the pool where Claude had caught her first fish, and where, as he stood by the water side, he seemed to feel her little hands clasping the rod with him as mentor, instructing her in the art.

But, try hard as he would, no salmon rose. Every pool, every eddy which had proved the home of some silvery fish in the past, was essayed in vain; and at last, after a

couple of hours' honest work, he gave it up
as a bad job, and determined to try at the
mouth of the river, just where the salt tide
met the fresh water, for one of the peel which
frequented that part.

Winding up his line, and hesitating as to
how he should fish, he walked swiftly back,
wondering whether Glyddyr would still be
on the bridge, waiting to insult him with
word and look, and feeling heartily relieved
to see that the place was clear.

Reaching the bridge, he went on down by
the river on the same side as that on which
he had been fishing.

There was no path there, and the way among
the rugged stones and bushes was laborious, but
he crept and leaped and climbed away till he
was within a hundred yards of the sea, where
the river began to change its rough, turbulent
course to one that was calm and gliding.

It was extremely tortuous here, and in
places there were eddies, in which patches of
foam floated, just as they had come down
from the little falls above, lingering, as it
were, before taking the irrevocable plunge

into the tide which would carry them far out to sea.

Close by one of these eddies, where the water looked black and dark, the fisher had to make his way down to the very edge of the river, to climb round a rugged point, and so reach the wilderness of boulders below, among which the river rushed hurriedly towards the bar.

It was the most slippery piece of climbing of all, and about half way along Chris was standing with one foot upon an isolated stone, the other on a ledge of slatey rock, about to make his final spring, when something floating on the surface of the still water took his attention.

It was only a scrap of pinkish paper, printed at the top, carefully ruled and crossed, and bearing some writing in coarse blue pencil.

Chris stared hard at the object, for it was a telegram. Glyddyr had received a telegram, crumpled it up and thrown it into the water, where, in all probability, consequent upon the action of the water, it had slowly opened out till it lay flat, as if asking to be read.

" Bah ! " ejaculated Chris, turning away from temptation—as it seemed to him.

The intention was good, but the mischief was done. Even as he glanced at the telegram lying there upon the water he took in its meaning. The writing was so large and clear, and the message so brief, that he grasped it all in what the Germans call an *augenblick*.

" *Back the Prince's filly.—Gellow.* "

A curious feeling of annoyance came over Chris as he climbed on—a feeling which made him pick up a couple of heavy stones, and dash them down one after the other into the river.

The second was unnecessary, for the first was so well aimed that it splashed right into the middle of the paper, and bore it down into the depths of the river beneath the rocky bank ; and Chris walked on towards the smiling sea, with those words fixed in his mind and standing out before him.

" *Back the Prince's filly.* "

The thing seemed quite absurd, and he felt more and more angry as he went a few yards farther and prepared his tackle, and began

to fish just in the eddy where the stream and
sea met. And there goodly fish, which had
come up with the tide to feed on the tasty
things brought down by the little river from
the high grounds, gave him plenty of opportunities for making his creel heavy, but he
saw nothing save the words upon the telegram, and could think of nothing else.

It was evidently a very important message
to Glyddyr about some race, but for the time
being he had no idea what race was coming
off. He was fond of sport in one way, but
Epsom, Ascot, Newmarket, Doncaster and
Goodwood had no charm for him.

But he knew accidentally that Glyddyr was
a man who betted heavily, and report said that
he won large sums on the turf, while by the
irony of fate here was he, possibly Glyddyr's
greatest enemy, suddenly put in possession
of one of his great turf secrets—undoubtedly
a hint from his agent by which he would win
a heavy sum.

"Well, let him win a heavy sum," cried
Chris petulantly, as if some one were present
tempting him to try his luck. "Let him win

and gamble and lose, and go hang himself; what is it to me?"

He hurriedly wound in his line, to find that a fish had hooked itself; but, in his petulant state, he gave the rod a sharp jerk, snatched the hook free, and began to retrace his way to the bridge; but before he reached the spot where he had had to step amid the big stones, he caught sight of a scrap of pink paper sailing down to meet the tide, and he could not help seeing the words,—

" *Prince's fil—*"

And directly after another ragged fragment floated by showing, at the torn edge where the stone had dashed through, the one mutilated word,—

" *Bac—*"

" Any one would think there were invisible imps waiting to tempt me," thought Chris. " How absurd !"

He strode on, leaping and climbing along the rugged bank till he once more reached the bridge, crossed it, and was half-way back to his apartments when he saw Gartram coming along the road with Claude and Mary.

His first instinct was to avoid them. The second, to go straight on and meet them, and this he did, to find that, as he raised his hat, Gartram turned away to speak to Claude, and completely check any attempt at recognition on her part.

" How contemptible ! " thought Chris. " Now, if I had been as well off as Glyddyr, I should have been seized by the hand, asked why I did not go up more to the Fort, and generally treated as if I were a son."

" *Back the Prince's filly.* "

The idea came with such a flash across his brain that he started and looked sharply over his shoulder to see if any one had spoken.

" How curious," he thought. " It just shows how impressionable the human mind is. If I gave way to it, I should begin calculating odds, and fooling away my pittance in gambling on the turf. I suppose every man has the gaming instinct latent within him, ready to fly into activity directly the right string is pulled. Ah, well, it isn't so with me."

He walked on, trying to think of how beautiful the day was, and how lovely the silver-

damascened sea, with the blue hills beyond ;
but away softly, describing arcs of circles with
the tips of her masts, lay Glyddyr's yacht, and
there, just before him, was Glyddyr himself
going into the little post office, where the one
wire from the telegraph pole seemed to descend
through the roof.

"Gone to send a message," thought Chris,
with a feeling of anger that he could not for
the moment analyse, but whose explanation
seemed to come the next moment. To back
the Prince's horse, perhaps make more thousands, and then—"Oh ! this is maddening !"
he said, half aloud ; and he increased his pace
till he reached the pretty cottage where he had
long been the tenant of a pleasant, elderly,
ship-captain's widow; and after hanging his rod
upon the hooks in the little passage, entered
his room, threw the creel into the corner, and
himself into a chair.

"Cut dead !" he exclaimed bitterly. "After
all these years of happy life, to be served like
that."

"*Back the Prince's filly.*"

The words seemed to stand out before him,

and he gave quite a start as the door opened
and the pleasant smiling face of his landlady
appeared, the bustling woman bearing in a
large clean blue dish.

" How many this time, Mr Lisle ? " she said.
" Of course you'll like some for dinner ? "

" What ? No ; none at all, Mrs Sarson,"
said Chris hastily.

" No fish, sir ? Why, James Gadby came
along and said that the river was just full."

" Yes ; I daresay, but I came back. Head-
ache. Not well."

" Let me send for Dr Asher, sir. There's nothing like taking things in time. A bit of cold,
perhaps, with getting yourself so wet wading."

" No, no, Mrs Sarson ; there's nothing the
matter. Please don't bother me now. I want
to think."

The woman went out softly, shaking her head.

" Poor boy ! " she said to herself ; " I know.
Things are not going with him as they should,
and it's a curious thing that love, as well
enough I once used to know."

" *Back the Prince's filly.*"

The words stood out so vividly before Chris

Lisle that he sprang from his seat, caught up a book, and threw himself back once more in a chair by the window to read.

But, as he turned over the leaves, he heard a familiar voice speaking in its eager, quick tones, and, directly after, there was another voice which seemed to thrill him through and through, the sounds coming in at the open window as the light steps passed.

" No, Mary dear. Let's go home."

There was a ring of sadness in the tone in which those words were uttered, which seemed to give Chris' hope. Claude could not be happy to speak like that.

He crept to the window, and, from behind the curtain, watched till he could see the white flannel dress with its blue braiding no more.

" If I were only rich," thought Chris ; and then he gave an angry stamp on the floor as he heard a quick pace, and saw Glyddyr pass, evidently hurrying on to overtake the two girls, who must have parted from Gartram lower down.

Half mad with jealousy, he made for the door, but only to stop with his fingers upon the handle, as he felt how foolish any such step would be, and, going back to his chair, he took up his book again, and opened it, and there before him the words seemed to start out from the page.

"*Back the Prince's filly.*"

He closed the book with an angry snap.

"Look here," he said to himself, "am I going to be ill, and is all this the beginning of a fit of delirium?"

He laughed the next instant, and then, as if obeying the strange impulse within him, he crossed the room and rang the bell.

"Have you taken away the newspaper that was here, Mrs Sarson?" he said sharply.

The pleasant face before him coloured up.

"I beg your pardon, sir. I didn't think you'd be back yet, and so I'd made so bold."

"Bring it back," said Chris sternly.

"Bless the poor man, what is coming to him?" muttered the landlady, as she hurried out to her own room. "He was once as amiable as a dove, and now nothing's right for him."

"Thank you; that will do," said Chris, shortly; and as soon as he was alone he stood with the paper in his hand.

CHAPTER XV.

TEMPTED.

It was some minutes before Chris opened that paper, and then he had to turn it over and over before he found the racing intelligence, and even then he did not begin to read, for plainly before him were the words,—

"*Back the Prince's filly.*"

Then in a quick, excited way he looked down the column he had found, and before long saw that the important race on the *tapis* was at Liverpool, and the last bettings on the various horses were before him, beginning with the favourite at four to one, and going on to horses against which as many as five hundred to one was the odds.

But the Prince's horse! What Prince? What horse? He stood thinking, and recalled a rumour which he had heard to the effect that the Prince's horses were run under the name

of Mr.Blanck, and there, sure enough, was in
the list far down :—

"Mr Blanck's ch. f. Simoom, 100 to 1."

Chris dashed down the paper in a rage.

"What have I to do with such things as
this?" he said aloud. "Even if I were a
racing man I could not do it. It is too dishonourable."

Then he set to work to argue the matter
out. He had come upon the information by
accident, and it might be perfectly worthless.
Even if the advice was good, the matter was
all speculation—a piece of gambling—and if a
man staked his money upon a horse it was the
merest chance whether this horse would win ;
so if he used the "tip," he would be wronging
no one, except, perhaps, himself, by risking
money he could not spare.

Anxiety, love, jealousy and disappointment
had combined to work Chris Lisle's brain into
a very peculiar state of excitement, and he
found himself battling hard now with a strange
sense of temptation.

Here was a message giving Glyddyr information how to make money, and it had fallen

into other hands. Why should not he, Christopher Lisle, seize the opportunity, take advantage of such a chance as might never come to him again, and back the Prince's horse to the extent of four or five hundred pounds? Poor as he called himself, he had more than that lying at his bankers; and if he won, it might be the first step towards turning the tables on Gartram, and winning Claude.

True, the information was meant for his rival, but what of that? All was fair in love and war. Glyddyr would stand at nothing to master him: so why should he shrink? It would be an act of folly, and like throwing away a chance.

Then his training stepped in, and did battle for him, pointing out that no gentleman would stoop to such an act, and for the next six hours a terrible struggle went on, which ended in honour winning.

"I would not do such a dirty action; and she would scorn me if I did," he said to himself. "Eh? Want me, Mrs Sarson?"

"Which it's taking quite a liberty, Mr Lisle, sir," said his landlady, who had come for the fifth time into his room; "but if you would let me send for Doctor Asher, it would ease my mind—indeed it would."

"Asher? Send for him? Are you ill?"

"I? No, my dear boy, but you are. You are quite feverish. It's terrible to see you. Not a bit of dinner have you tasted, and you've been walking up and down the room as if you had the toothache, for hours. Now, do trust to me, my dear, an old motherly body like me; I'd better send for him."

"My dear Mrs Sarson, he could not do me the least good," said Chris, smiling at the troubled face before him. "It was a fit of worry, that's all; but it's better now—all gone. There, you see, I'm quite calmed down now, and you shall prescribe for me. Give me some tea and meat together."

"But are you really better, my dear?"

"Yes; quite right now."

"And quite forgive me for calling you my dear, Mr Lisle, sir? You are so like my son out in New Zealand, and you have been with me so long."

"Forgive you? Yes."

"That's right," said the woman, beginning to beam; and hurrying in and out she soon had a comfortable-looking and tempting meal spread waiting before her lodger's eager eyes, and he made a determined attack upon that before him.

"That's more like you, Mr Lisle," she said, smiling her satisfaction.

"Would you mind opening the window a little more, Mrs Sarson?" said Chris, as he drove the Prince's horse right out of his mind; and races, jockeys, grand stands, and even Glyddyr faded from his heated brain.

"Certainly, sir. And what a lovely evening it is—beautiful. Hah! there goes that Mr Glyddyr's boat off to his yacht; and there's Mr Gartram in it, and the young ladies. Going for an evening sail, I suppose."

Chris dropped his knife and fork upon his plate.

"Bless me!" ejaculated the landlady, turning sharply round.

"Nothing, nothing, Mrs Sarson," said Chris hastily; "that will do now. I'll ring. Don't wait."

The landlady looked at him curiously, and left the room ; and as soon as she was gone, Chris sprang from his chair, took a binocular glass from where it hung in its case against the wall, focussed it, and fixed it upon the smart gig being rowed out on the bright water.

" I've fought all I knew, and I'm beaten," he muttered, as he saw Glyddyr leaning towards Claude, and talking to her. "Every man has his temptations, and the best and strongest fall if the temptation is too strong. I am only a poor, weak, blundering sort of fellow, I suppose; and I've fallen—low—very low indeed.

"Claude, my darling !" he groaned, as he lowered the glass and gazed wistfully out toward the boat, "if it were some good, true fellow whom you loved, and I was going to see you happy, I'd try and bear it all like a man. But you can't be happy with a fast scoundrel like that ; and you love me. I know, I'm sure you do, and I'd do anything to save you from such a fate."

He pitched the glass on to the sofa, took a time table from where it lay, and, after satisfy-ing himself as to the hours of the trains, he went quickly towards the door, just as it was opened and Mrs Sarson appeared.

"There, my dear," she said, holding up a large glass dish; "there's a junket of which any woman might be proud, and—"

"No, no; not now, Mrs Sarson. I'm going out."

"Going out, sir?"

"Yes; up to London."

"To London, sir?"

"Yes; for a day or two," and he hurried by her.

Half-an-hour later, he was on his way in the town fly to the railway station, just as the sun, low down in the west, was shining full on the white sails of Glyddyr's yacht, as it glided slowly on over the bright, calm sea.

Chris turned his eyes away, and looked straight before him as he mentally conjured up the gathered thousands—the bright green course, the glossy horses making their preliminary canter, with the gay silken jackets of the jockeys filling out as they rose in their stirrups, and flashing in the bright sunshine. There was the trampling of hoofs over the springy turf, the starting as the flag was dropped, the dashing of one to the front, of others challenging, and the minutes of excitement as, in a gathering roar, one horse seemed to glide out from a compressed group, gradually increasing its distance as it sped.

Hiss, rush, roar! Then the vision had passed away, and Chris Lisle was seated, not in a saddle, but on a cushion in a first-class carriage, the speed increasing and the wind rushing by the windows as, with cheeks flushed, he rode on, his teeth set, and completely now under the domination of one thought alone as he softly repeated to himself the words he had read upon the telegram,—

" Back the Prince's filly,"

and a few minutes later the figures he had seen in that day's news,—

" 100 to 1."

The simoom seemed to be scorching up his brains.

It was all one whirl of excitement to Chris Lisle—that railway journey to town, and there were moments when he asked himself whether

he was sane to go upon such a mission. The
night journey of the train seemed like a race,
and the rattle of the bridges and tunnels sug-
gested the shouts and cheers of the crowd as
the horses swept on. But he had determined
to persevere, and with stubborn determination
he went on, reached town, and without hesitation laid his money—four hundred pounds, in
four different sums so as to insure himself
as well as he could, in each case getting the
odds of 100 to 1, so that, should the Prince's
horse come in first, he would be the winner of
forty thousand pounds.

As soon as this was done, he went to a quiet
hotel to try and get some rest.

But that was impossible, for he was face to
face with his folly. Four hundred pounds gone
in an insane hope of winning forty thousand,
and he could see now how absurd it was.

"Never mind," he said bitterly; "I shall
not be the first fool who has lost money on a
race, and I shall have had the excitement of
a bit of gambling."

His idea was to stay in town and go to a
theatre, so as to divert the current of his

thoughts ; then have a long night's rest and go to some other place of amusement the next day, so as to pass the time till the race had been run, and he knew the worst.

He dined, or rather tried to dine, and for the first time in his life drank heavily, but the wine seemed not to have the slightest effect.

Then in a feverish heat he went to one of the best theatres, and saw a social drama en-acted by the people who filled his brain, what was going on upon the stage being quite a blank.

He saw himself as a disappointed hero, and Glyddyr, as the successful man, carrying all before him, winning Claude's love, and then, in what seemed to be the last act, there was a wedding, and a wretched man going after-wards right along to one of the towering cliffs overhanging the sea, below Danmouth, and leaping off to end his woes.

"I'm glad I came to the theatre," he said mockingly to himself, in one of his lucid in-tervals. "Better have gone to a doctor for something to send me to sleep."

Then he became conscious of the fact that people in the pit were saying "Hush!" and

" Sit down ! " and that somebody had risen and come out from the place where he was jammed in, right in the centre of the stalls, just as the climax of the play was being reached.

Then he grew conscious that he was the offender, and breathed more freely as he got out into the cool night air.

It was not ten, and he found a chemist's open near the Strand.

" I'm not very well," he said to the gentle-manly-looking man behind the counter. " Had a lot of trouble, made me restless, and I want to take something to give me a good night's rest. Can you give me a dose of laudanum ? "

The man looked at him curiously.

" You ought to go to a doctor," he said.

" Doctor ! Absurd ! What for ? I'm as well as you are. Give me something calming. It will be better than going back to the hotel and taking brandy or wine."

The chemist nodded, and prepared a draught.

" What's that ? Laudanum—morphia ? "

" No ; a mild dose of chloral. Try it. If it does not act as you wish, I should advise you to go to a physician in the morning."

Chris nodded, took the bottle, and strolled back to his hotel, where he at once went to bed after swallowing his draught.

It did not have the desired effect. His idea was to take a draught which would plunge him in oblivion for a few hours ; but this dose of chloral seemed to transport him to a plain, surrounded by mountains covered with the most gloriously-tinted foliage, where flowers rippled all over the meadow - like pastures, and cascades of the most brilliant iridescent waters came foaming down, sparkling in the glorious sunshine.

All deliciously dreamy and restful, but when the morning came it did not seem to him that he had slept. Still, he was calmer, and felt more ready to think out the inevitable.

" How many hours shall I have to wait ? " he said.

The race would probably be run about three o'clock, and till then he must be as patient as he could.

" Better go back at once," he thought, " and repent at leisure over my madness.'

But he did not, for he accepted the last

suggestion of his brain, partook of a hurried breakfast, and jumped into a hansom ; had himself driven to the station, and soon after was being borne away by the express.

The rest of that day's proceedings were a dreamy whirl of confusion. The rushing noise of the train seemed to bring back the old excitement, and this increased as he reached the station, and had himself driven to the course, where one of the first things he learned was that the case was hopeless ; for the horse he had backed had gone down in the betting, till two hundred to one could be obtained, and for the first time he felt sick at heart.

He went up into the principal stand, securing a good place to see the race, and waited while two others were run, the horses flying by without exciting the slightest interest ; the only satisfaction he gained was in having them pass, so as to be nearer to the great feature of the day.

At last, just as he had pictured it from old recollections of a minor race he had once seen, there was the shouting and bawling of the odds, the clearing of the course, and then the preliminary canter of the ten competitors, among which he now made out the colours of Simoom, a big ordinary looking horse, with nothing to draw attention to it, while the three first favourites of the *cognoscenti* were the perfection of equine beauty, and their admirers shouted with excitement as they flashed by.

Then, after five false starts, each of which was maddening to Chris, who, while thinking the worst, could not help a gleam of hope piercing the dark cloud which overshadowed him, the cry arose that they were off, and amid a babel of sounds, as the parti-coloured throng of jockeys swept along the green course and disappeared, spasmodic cries arose, "Lady Ronald," "Safflower—Safflower leads," "Rotten race," "The favourite shows 'em all her heels," "Look! The favourite!"

The horses, after a period of silence, had swept round into sight again, and it was seen that three were together, then there was an interval, and there were four, another interval, and the rest behind.

The second group excited no notice, save

from Chris, who made out that his horse was with them; and while every eye was fixed on the exciting race between the favourite and the two horses which strove hard to get abreast, there was suddenly a yell of excitement, for Simoom all at once shot out from among the second lot, and going well, with her jockey using neither whip nor spur, began rapidly to near the leaders.

The shouts increased, and a thrill ran through Chris as he saw the plain-looking mare glide on, but apparently too late to overtake the others.

Another roar as it was seen that the favourite's jockey was beginning to use his whip, and the roar increased as Safflower was level with her shoulder, was head to head, was head in front, and the next moment, hopelessly beaten, the favourite was passed by Lady Ronald as well, who now challenged Safflower, and they were racing level for fifty yards.

The excitement grew frantic. " Safflower! Lady Ronald! Safflower! Safflower!"

" No, no, no!" shouted a man on Chris's left. " Look!"

Chris heard all he said, and stood there bending forward, his lips apart, and eyes starting, as if turned to stone, living a very life in those seconds, as, amid a roar like the rushing of the tempest itself, the contemned mare came on.

" By George, sir, if the course had been a hundred yards more, she'd have won," roared the man on Chris's left. " Safflower's done. It's Lady Ronald ; by ——, no. Hurrah ! Simoom ! Simoom !" and in the midst of the frantic excitement, the mare upon which Chris's hopes were fixed passed Safflower. There was a quick touch of the whip and she was alongside of Lady Ronald, and then Simoom's nose showed in front, and in the next few bounds she was half-a-length ahead, and swept past the post—winner.

The man on Chris's left suddenly seized his arm.

" Hurrah for the dark horse," he cried. " Just for the fun of the thing, I put a sov. on her, and I've won two hundred pounds. I beg your pardon, sir, I see you're hit. Forgive my excitement. Don't be down-hearted ; come and have a glass of champagne.

" Thank you," said Chris quietly ; but he did not move, for the place seemed to be spinning round him, and he held tightly by the rails till a hand was laid upon his arm.

" Can I help you ? You look ill."

" Help me ? No ; I'm all right now," said Chris, making an effort. " It was so sudden."

" Have you lost heavily ? "

" Lost ? " said Chris, looking at him wildly. " No ; I've won."

He felt his hand being shaken warmly, and then he sank back into a wild, confused dream, in the midst of which he knew that he was being borne back by one of the express trains, with the roar of the race in his ears, and the sight of the horses sweeping by before his eyes.

As he neared town he began to grow more calm, and he found himself repeating the words,—

" Forty thousand pounds ! I've won ; but shall I win her now ? "

And then, like a dark cloud, came the recollection of how he had obtained the information upon which his success was based.

" I can never name it to a soul," he muttered. " I must have been mad."

CHAPTER XVI.

GARTRAM TAKES HIS DOSE.

" It's all right, I tell you, my dear boy. You don't understand women yet. A girl who says *snap* the moment you say *snip*, isn't worth having. A good, true woman takes some wooing and winning ; and no wonder, for it is a tremendous surrender for her to make."

" Yes, sir, you are quite right, but—"

" Yes ; never mind the buts, Glyddyr. I could put my foot down, and say : 'Claude, my dear, there's your husband,' but it would mean a scene, and a lot of excitement, and I should be ill—perhaps have one of my confounded fits."

" But without going so far as that, sir, couldn't you—just a little, you know—parental authority—you understand. I am kept back so terribly as yet."

" No, my lad, I should not be serving your cause," said Gartram firmly. " You see, she

had always been so intimate with that fellow
Lisle. Boy and girl together. It will take a
little time to wean her from the fancy, and if
I pull out the authoritative stop I shall be
making him into a hero and her into a persecuted heroine. I may as well tell you that
she is a bit firm, like I am, and any angry
discussion on my part would perhaps make
her stubborn."

"Then, perhaps, you had better not speak,
sir."

"Decidedly not. There, you have the run
of my place. Set to and win her like a man.
Get along with you, you dog. Smart, handsome fellow like you don't want any help. It's
only a matter of time. Don't seem to push
your suit too hard. Treat it all as a something
settled; and all you have to do is to get her
used to you and her position as your betrothed.
Bah! it will all come right, so don't let's risk
opposition. You will win."

"You are right, sir," said Glyddyr. "I'll
be patient."

"Of course you will. That's right. I say,
though, that little upset?"

" Little upset, sir ? " said Glyddyr starting.

" I mean about your friend, the visitor from town, whose wife came after him."

" Oh ! " exclaimed Glyddyr. " I didn't know what you meant."

" Rather an exciting affair, that. Strikes me that if it had had a tragic termination, your friend would not have broken his heart. I say, here you are in a hurry to get married, and you never know how the lady may turn out."

" Ah, that was an exception, sir," said Glyddyr hurriedly.

" Yes ; but depend upon it, my dear boy, that was a hasty marriage. The gentleman said *snip*, and she said *snap*. Wasn't it so ? "

" Yes ; I think you are right," said Glyddyr.

" What a temper that woman must have. They tell me she deliberately stepped off the pier to follow him, or drown herself in a fit of passion."

" Well, I'll take your advice, sir," said Glyddyr, hurriedly changing the conversation. " Of course, I can't help feeling impatient."

" No, of course, no," said Gartram. " Come

in," he added, as there was a timid knock at the door.

"I beg pardon, sir, but Doctor Asher said I was to be particular as to time."

Sarah Woodham entered the room with a small tray, bearing glass and bottle.

There was a peculiar, shrinking, furtive look about the woman, that would have impressed a stranger unfavourably; but Glyddyr was too intent upon his own business, and Gartram already disliked his old servant, and did not shrink about showing it.

"Oh!" he said roughly. "Well, pour it out. Won't take a glass, I suppose, Glyddyr?"

"Oh, no, thanks. Not my favourite bin."

"Thank your stars. Nice thing to be under the doctor's hands. Hard, isn't it? Regular piece of tyranny."

"Oh, you'll soon get over that, Mr Gartram. Temporary trouble."

"Ah, I don't know, my lad. Here, that's more than usual, isn't it, Sarah?"

"No, sir. Exactly the quantity."

"Humph! Bah! Horrible!"

He had gulped the medicine down, and thrust the glass back on the tray.

" There, take it away," he said.

The woman looked at him furtively, and slowly left the room.

" How I do hate to see a nurse in black," exclaimed Gartram impatiently. " When a man's ill, the woman who attends upon him ought to look bright and cheerful. That woman always gives me a chill."

" Why not make her dress differently ? "

" Can't. Widow of that poor fellow who was killed."

" Oh, yes ; I remember."

" Whim of Claude's to have her here."

" Yes, I know. Your old servant. Well, it was a graceful act on Miss Gartram's part."

" Of course ; but it worries me."

" The medicine makes you feel a little irritable, perhaps."

" No, it does not, man. It's tonic, and I'm taking chloral, which is calming, or I don't know what I should do."

" Chloral ? " said Glyddyr.

" Yes ; curse it—and bless it. I don't know

what I should do without it. Tell you what'
though. You must give me some more sails
in your yacht. Cuts both ways?"

" I shall be most happy."

" Yes ; does me good and gives you pleasant opportunities, eh ? I ought to be ashamed
to say it, perhaps, but I am not. Confound
that medicine ! What a filthy taste it does
leave in one's mouth ; quite makes one's throat
tingle, too."

" When will you have another sail, sir ? "

" Oh, I don't know. When did we go
last ? "

" Tuesday."

" To be sure ; and this is Thursday. That
medicine seems to confuse me a bit sometimes.
Well, say this evening. By-the-bye, Glyddyr,
that was a pleasant little idea of yours."

- " What idea, sir ?"

" Quite startled my girl when that puss
Mary drew her attention to it. How cunning
you young fellows grow now-a-days."

" I don't quite grasp what you mean, sir."

" Altering the name of the yacht."

" Oh ! "

" A very delicate little compliment, my lad, and it does you credit."

" But Miss Gartram, sir ? " said Glyddyr hurriedly ; " is she in the drawing-room ? "

" In the drawing-room ? no," said Gartram, with a strange display of irritability. "I told you when you first came that she had gone for a long walk up the glen with her cousin."

" I beg your pardon, sir. I don't think—"

" Now, damn it all, Glyddyr, don't you take to contradicting me ; and perhaps by this time that confounded scoundrel Lisle has followed her."

Glyddyr leaped from his seat.

" No, no ; I don't mean it," said Gartram, calming down. " Lisle is not at home. Gone to London, I think, or I wouldn't have let them go. There, my lad, don't you take any notice of me," he continued, holding out his hand ; " it's that medicine. I wish Asher was hung. So sure as I take a dose, I grow irritable and snappish, just as if a fit was threatening ; but it keeps 'em off, eh ? "

" I should say so, decidedly ; and I wouldn't dwell upon the possibility if I were you."

" Well, curse it all, man, who does ? " cried
Gartram fiercely. " There, I beg your pardon.
Go and meet the girls and come back, and we'll
have an early dinner, and then you can take us
for a sail. Well, what the devil do you want ? "
he roared, as Sarah re-entered the room ;
" haven't I just taken the cursed stuff ? "

" Beg pardon, sir, a telegram."

" Well, don't stand staring like a black
image. Give it to me."

" For Mr Glyddyr, sir—the boy heard from
the sailors at the pier that he was here, and
brought it on."

" Well, then, give it to him ; and look here,
I'm sure you must have given me too strong a
dose this morning."

" No, sir ; Miss Claude measured it before
she went. I took the bottle and glass to her."

" Humph ! Feels wrong somehow. Is it
fresh stuff ? "

" No, sir ; the same."

" Humph ! Well, Glyddyr, good news ? "

" Ye—es," said Glyddyr, with a peculiar
look in his eyes. " Only from my agent in
town. You'll excuse me now ? "

" To be sure. Go round by the bridge and you'll meet 'em. Dinner at five. Hi, Sarah ! Mind that : five."

" Yes, sir," said the woman, and she glided like a black shadow out of the room after Glyddyr, who hurried along the terrace down to the beach, where he could light a cigar and smoke.

" I feel as if they were poisoning me amongst them," said Gartram quite savagely. " Not trying to put me out of the way, are they, for the sake of my coin ? How I do hate to see that woman going about like a great black cat. Bah ! I'm as full of fancies as a child."

Glyddyr lit his cigar and took out his telegram again and read it.

" *My congratulations. Hope you put it on heavy. I did. Coming down.—Gellow.*"

The curse which Glyddyr uttered was, metaphorically speaking, glowing enough to fuse the sand.

The next minute he began walking swiftly along under the towering granite cliffs, so as to get out of sight and hearing while he gave vent to his feelings, for he felt that he could not command himself.

The telegram meant so much.

"I shall have to kill that man before I have done. Yes; I shall have to kill that man," said Glyddyr.

He started and looked up, for, plainly heard, some one seemed to repeat his words, "Kill that man."

"Bah!" he cried impatiently, as he looked in the direction from which the sounds came, to find he was facing a huge wall of rock. "Frightened at echoes now!"

END OF VOL. I.

COLSTON AND COMPANY, PRINTERS, EDINBURGH.

www.ingramcontent.com/pod-product-compliance
Lightning Source LLC
Chambersburg PA
CBHW031400020726
47499CB00005B/1461